BUTTERFLIES

A LOVE STORY WITH A GUN IN ITS MOUTH

BUTTERFLIES

A LOVE STORY WITH A GUN IN ITS MOUTH

MACKENZIE KALISH

I dedicate this book to my family and friends.
If it were not for each of you affecting
my life in some way or another, good or bad,
supportive or detrimental, this story would
simply not exist.

A special thanks needs to be made to Andrew Le, for the cover art, design, and artistic input.

Shea Sjoberg, for the helping hand with design, layout, and custom number typography.

Maya Zohbi, whose artistic vision helped lead me to the final product of this book.

My parents, for continuing to stand by me, and support me, even when I have made that the more difficult choice.

My friends, I am eternally grateful for each and every one of you. Thank you for everything, each of you inspires me in some way or another.

"So what is love?
A feeling that we make up
A parallel to drugs
I swear I'll never wake up
I'm everything she was
I swear we'll never make up
She's lying like a rug
Everyday is a war
And I'm just dying to tug"

— LVE

TABLE OF CONTENTS

PROLOGUE

I've always heard people say that suicide is the easy way out, but let me tell you, it is actually quite difficult. "I can do this," I think to myself, in a dark, dark sense of encouragement. My lips are wrapped around the barrel of a .38 special revolver and my hand is trembling. I keep getting distracted by the cold metal against my lips and the end of the barrel pushing against the roof of my mouth. I try to let my mind go blank and really focus on how I'm going to be able to press down on the trigger, but it's not as simple as I always thought it would be. I'm not sure if I'm ready to die, and the idea that I might want to live is really holding me back from letting myself go. I've always been a worrier, but this time, the time I don't want to have any second thoughts, I do. I guess it makes sense, seeing as death is such a permanent thing, but I really wish my stubborn ass would just get on board with the rest of me that doesn't want to breathe for another second.

"What happens when you die?" I ask myself. I think of all the myths I've heard about the experience and settle on, "you see your whole life flash before your eyes."

The problem is that when I look back at my life, I tend to remember the bad over the good. I'm not an extremely negative person or anything like that, but left to my own devices, I would definitely fall into the category of cynical people. I have always felt that an artist, which I obnoxiously consider myself to be, thrives in a state of misery and heartbreak. This is an extremely unhealthy thought process to grow in, but that never stopped me from doing it. The idea that I work better when I'm miserable or heartbroken has influenced every decision I have ever made. The worst part about it is, it has always proven accurate. If you ask me, I think that every great song, film, and piece of art were created out of someone's heartbreak.

Heartbreak fascinates me. Possibly because it's something I've grown so accustomed to, or it could just be because it's such a powerful emotion. Regardless of the reason why, it intrigues me, it always has. The idea of heartbreak seems so foolish, but go ask anyone who's gone through it, and I promise you, they'll tell you there's nothing worse.

The funny thing about having your heart broken is that the impact it has on you depends solely on your definition of the term itself. Love is love, and what you make love mean will determine who you are in this world.

I desperately wish that the first time I heard about the power of love, I wasn't too young to register it. I wish someone could have told me to watch out, or be careful of those silly four letters that control everything in this world, but, like every other child, a concept so great can't be understood until it is felt. I know children feel love, and from the day you are born, you love your parents, and things like that, but that's not the kind of love I'm talking about. The love I'm referring to is the kind of love that doesn't let you sleep at night. The kind of love that fills empty glasses with whiskey, stuffs ashtrays with cigarette butts until they spill out onto tables, and keeps self-help books in the aisles of stores world wide. The kind of love you wish you had never felt, but wouldn't trade the experience for anything in this world.

When I try to imagine my life flashing before my eyes, all I can see is her, and the old me, and a past that I need to shed. Love has made me who I am today, which is weird because this is the second time I have had a gun in my mouth.

Like most people, I found my first love as a teenager, and that's sort of where my life began to spiral downward. I'm twenty-nine now, and I've only just begun to feel like an adult. Some may say that people mature during puberty, or in college, but I think it takes most people fifteen years to truly mature. The time between the ages of fifteen and thirty really shape who you become in this world. The experiences you have during those years are generally the biggest, most important, and most valuable of a person's life. At least that is the truth for the only person I can really speak for: myself.

So here I am, literally trying to talk myself to death. I feel like such a cliché. It seems like it should be so easy, but now that I'm sitting here, I realize that not one muscle, it doesn't matter how strong it may be, can pull that trigger. The trigger of a gun that you hold to your own head is pulled with your brain.

Maybe this is why people leave suicide notes. Maybe writing it all down just before lets you air out a bit. You leave everything on that piece of paper, and don't have to sift through it all in your head.

The letter itself almost seems like a cop-out to me, though. If you leave a note, you're doing it because you know that whoever finds it is sure as hell going to hold on to it.

Someone's suicide note is not something that gets accidentally recycled with that week's coupons to the local grocery store. A suicide note is the kind of thing that people keep strategically hidden under miscellaneous items in desk drawers for the rest of their lives. When you leave a piece of physical evidence like that, you do not really want to die. You'll be remembered forever, at least by a few, because when they hear what your note said, those words will never be able to escape from their mind. They will haunt people forever, and that's just downright unfair. That is precisely why I refuse to go along with the public's pre-conceived notions of how a suicide is supposed to happen. The people my suicide note would be left to have already heard it. Whether it's "I love you" or "fuck you," I take solace in knowing that my suicide note has been scattered in arguments, speeches, proclamations of love, broken text messages, and vows over the last fifteen years.

"Damn!" I think to myself. "That sounded amazing." I'm the kind of asshole that sometimes gets impressed by the way my thoughts sound in my own head, and that was one of those times.

I finally feel like I've summed up exactly how I feel about the situation, and now I need to make my choice. I can either be a coward and dramatically throw this gun across the room, hoping maybe it will fire and somehow ricochet off something and hit me, or I can just man up and do it.

"Here goes nothing," says the voice in my head. I take one final breath and clench my eyes tight. As I hear the halfway click of the trigger, I brace myself for the explosion that is about to be released from the pistol. When I feel the trigger actually hit the handle of the gun, however fast it may have happened, everything really does flash before my eyes...

My name is Thomas Doheny, and for all intents and purposes, I had a fairly normal childhood. I played on all the little league teams, went to summer camp, etc. I was never too good at sports, but I always liked the idea of them. Unfortunately, I was never the kid hitting home runs or throwing touchdown passes. I was always the kid you could find in the outfield, trying to catch moths and butterflies in my mitt. I could always find the four-leaf clover on a soccer field, but I couldn't exactly score.

As I got older, I gave up on all of the team sports and began doing stuff on my own. I found skateboarding when I was eight years old, and loved the non-team aspect of it. Skateboarding introduced me to my closest friend, too — a kid named Matt Miller, who grew up down the street from me. Matt and I went through everything together: we took every phase, or habit, or dilemma, head on, side-by-side.

It wasn't until I was in high school that my passion for skateboarding began to die out. As freshmen, Matt and I used skateboarding to meet a core group of friends, but we all slowly faded away from the sport together.

By the time I was a sophomore in high school, I started to have a social life outside of the skate park, and it was everything I had dreamed it would be. I went to a small school in the San Fernando Valley, and being that it was a brand new school, there were a lot of kinks that the school had not worked out yet. My first two years there, no security was present at all. Schools across the country are considered to be "Drug-Free Zones," at least that's what the signs say across their campuses. My school felt a lot more like a "Free-Drug Zone."

My sophomore year was when I really started partying, and it quickly got the best of me. I had smoked a joint before when I was much younger, or snuck a beer with my buddies, but it wasn't until high school that it all really became accessible.

I was never one for pills or hard drugs of any kind back then, but I sure did love my liquor. I was never smooth with girls, or carefree in social situations, until I figured out who I became after a few beers. I fell in love with the transformation I would undergo. All my angsty, fifteen-year-old stuff would disappear.

The fast-paced world of teenage partying excited me so much when I was first introduced to it, that it quickly replaced skateboarding for all my friends and me. Much like a lot of kids in America, every weekend quickly became about finding the address for a house party that night, finding a way there, and getting far too intoxicated. Teenagers, by nature, search for opportunities to feel independent. That's what partying offered us kids, and we all fell head-over-heels for it. As soon as someone's parents went out of town, everybody knew it. The inevitable trouble a kid was going to get into never out-weighed the opportunity to be the star of the night.

I know I'm not a part of the first generation to have kids partying in high school, and I know I won't be the last, but I feel pretty confident in the fact that I came from a generation that really raised the bar. I can't really speak for the rest of America because I come from one of the most ridiculous and sought-after cities in the world, but I'll tell you, growing up in Southern California was just fantastic.

I hate to sound like an asshole, and this is based off no facts or even personal experiences, but I'm pretty sure Los Angeles' party scene is one of the most destructive in the world to its kids. Don't get me wrong. I love my city more than almost anything, but it seems like it is hell-bent on destroying its youth. The amount of shit that has happened to me, my peers, and other kids in this city could easily be labeled a tragedy.

By the time I was halfway through my sophomore year, my average weekend went like this: I would wake up, eat breakfast, and leave the house around noon. I would go to a local store that never carded kids for tobacco and buy a pack of Camels. I would meet up with friends from school and we would get high.

Once we were all stoned, we would either jump on a bus and adventure to downtown, or play video games at someone's house. Once nighttime rolled around, we would have found the address to a party, and we would find a way there. On the way, we would try to get alcohol, but we were still young enough that this was not an easy task. The best method to obtain beer was usually to send the hottest, most developed female of the group to the front of a liquor store and have her ask the loneliest looking guy. Was this dangerous? Sure. Was it irresponsible of not only us, but the poor sucker who thinks a fifteen-year-old is hot? Sure. But Beer!

We would get to the party, and it felt like a different world. We would drink beers, smoke weed, and listen to loud music until the cops came and broke it up. We would somehow always find a ride home, and usually all crash at the house of a friend whose parents were cool enough to think, "we were young once, too."

We all pretty much went to the same places and knew the same people. We all got our weed from a guy nicknamed "8-Ball" who lived in Matt's apartment building, and our cigarettes from the same foreign guy at the smoke shop, whom I'm pretty sure didn't know it was illegal to sell tobacco to minors.

8-Ball had lived in Matt's apartment building for years, and as we got older, he started to talk to us more and more. Now that we were fifteen, when 8-Ball would see us, he would smoke us out. 8-Ball was actually quite wise, and despite his terrifying, fully tattooed physique, he really looked out for us kids, and taught us lessons about mistakes he had made, that we should stray away from. The advice he gave us could easily be written off, though, because his words were passed to us alongside a blunt, but I've always been one to take things to heart.

One Sunday morning, Matt and I were leaving his apartment where we had crashed the night before and 8-Ball was leaning inside the passenger seat of a car in front of the building. We stood there watching for a second until 8-Ball finally noticed us. He said goodbye to the driver and walked back over to where we were. He greeted us and asked how our night was. He lightly punched both of us in the arm when he found out we brought no girls back and told us we "needed to step up our game." We, just like most fifteen-year-old boys, had no "game." He asked us if we wanted to smoke, and we both eagerly nodded our confirmations.

He pulled out a blunt and lit it, passing it to Matt first. Matt caught everyone off guard when he asked who the driver of the car was that 8-Ball was just talking to. 8-Ball thought for a minute before he took the blunt back out of my hand and began to puff on it again. He told us that he'd tell us, but that we could not repeat it or tell anybody. He explained to us that things were starting to get rough for him monetarily, and that he picked up a side job. Whereas some people's side jobs involve waiting tables, or serving coffee, 8-Ball's side job involved moving large amounts of cocaine. He told us it was something he hadn't done in years, but that he had another baby on the way, and he needed to bring in more money.

I don't know how I hadn't put his nickname and possible profession together before, but it finally all clicked. An eight ball is a slang term for one eighth of an ounce of cocaine. I remember being surprised by this information, but looking back now, I don't know why. 8-Ball was tattooed from head to toe and looked like he may or may not have killed people before.

If I had run into him anywhere else, I would have shit bricks, but I knew 8-Ball in a way that made him a distorted role model for me. I may have thought I was tough, or a badass at fifteen, but I was actually so naïve that this information 8-Ball said to me left me disillusioned about him. I felt so let down until he quickly reminded me of why I had looked up to him and thought he was so wise.

— "Listen here," he said between slow pulls from the blunt. "Life is messy. I've done some shit in my day that I would never repeat to you youngin's. Things that would make you sick to your stomach. The world is going to throw things at you left and right as you grow up, and you just have to be stronger than anything that may hit you. You have to find something you love and hold on to that shit, because it's the only thing that will ever really matter. I got a little baby girl, another on the way, and a wife. I'm fuckin' up for them right now. I know it's a mistake, but I'm going back to the only thing I know. Keep it straight from the get go, and you won't find yourself in situations like this. When you find the love of your life, you'll never let anything else take priority for you."

— "How do you know if something is the love of your life?" I asked him after a few seconds.

— "You get butterflies and all that wack shit," he told me. "I vowed I'd never start slangin' again, but if my baby needs to eat, my baby is going to eat. You'll meet someone, someday, who will make you rethink everything. She'll make you go back on promises, make new ones, and totally abandon your sense of independence. You'll know it's the love of your life because it will scare the shit out of you."

I let in what he was telling me, and remember thinking how deep it sounded. I would, of course, not really know what 8-Ball meant that day, until many years later.

Even though partying seemed to be all anyone my age cared about, we were all actually just kids, and still had to go back to school every Monday. I was always a smart kid; I just never really tried that hard. I was the type of student who would fail a test, but as soon as I was actually interested in a subject, I'd be raising my hand, doing all the homework, acing the tests, etc. English was always my favorite subject. I could not do math for the life of me, but words I could understand. I used school pretty much to socialize. I have always joked that my school was like a day camp, because it really was. I'd show up late, leave after a class or two to smoke a cigarette, or smoke some weed, come back for lunch, and half ass another class or two, and then I'd be done. I knew kids in other schools who would complain about the amount of work they had, and how tough school was, but I never saw it. I was always a fast talker and I could think on my feet, so if I ever really ran into any trouble at school, I would just sweet talk my way out of it. One of my proudest moments in high school was talking my grade up from a C to an A in my sophomore geometry class.

My parents, however, knew the importance of school and always tried to keep me on track. They were very lenient on my rules, but kept me in line. I know so many parents who were over-protective of their children, and it quickly backfired on them.

The kids who were sheltered their whole lives are usually the ones who end up really messing up when they get a taste of freedom. The kids who were never at a house party in high school are the same kids who were throwing up on the street and passed out their freshman year of college. My parents' approach to raising me was much looser than that. They always let me do what I wanted for the most part, as long as I kept the other shit in my life in order. If I kept up in school, did chores around the house, and never burned the candle at both ends too badly, they could care less that I was growing up too fast. In a world where we are exposed to everything so young, having to make your own boundaries is very important. I always had enough slack in the rope to know where I had to draw the line.

Aside from starting to drink and smoke and think that I was an adult, fifteen was actually a pretty boring year. At the time, I thought I was the coolest guy in the world, but, in retrospect, when I look back now, I was just a dumb kid.

The only thing that happened to me that year that really stuck was that one ill-fated day at school where I first saw Taylor Reid. Taylor Reid was just touring the campus of my high school when I first spotted her. I thought she was cute at first glance, but she didn't sweep me off my feet, or any of those old clichés. I went on with my day, and didn't see her again for a couple months.

When I got back from winter break, Taylor was starting that semester at my school. I saw her on my first day back and remembered having seen her before break when she was touring. I ended up having my fourth period class with her, which was a computer sciences class. At lunch I saw that she was sitting with people I knew, and when I walked over to the table, I was introduced to Taylor for the first time. I thought nothing of it really and went on with my day. I wish I had known in that moment that Taylor was going to be the most important person that ever entered my life. I wish some sort of alarm had gone off to make me aware that this girl was going to change me forever, but no bells or whistles were to be found. I, along with everyone else I knew, were unfortunately not psychic, so, at the time, this friendly encounter didn't seem like a future train wreck waiting to happen; it just seemed like lunch.

Over the course of the rest of that semester, Taylor and I actually became pretty close friends. We had that computer class together, which pretty much meant the two of us just talked and snuck out of school to smoke cigarettes everyday from ten to eleven. We hung out after school a few times because of mutual friends we had, but for the most part, our friendship was confined to that room in the science building of my school. That class, and Taylor, quickly became what I looked forward to each day.

Sixteen is a big year for anybody. At least it always seems like it at the time. My birthday lands right as school gets out every year. This year, my birthday actually landed on the day we all got out for summer. My dad was out of town at the time, and I somehow convinced my mother to let me throw a party at our house. Not only did I manage to convince my mom to let me throw the party, I convinced her to buy the alcohol. I was really on top of my shit that day, apparently.

Much like any house party that a teenager tries to throw, the "no more than thirty" quickly turns into over a hundred people, and it happens so quickly you can't put a stop to it. Whether someone asks to come and you realize how horrible it would be for you to say "no," or someone you barely know says they are bringing "a bunch of hot girls!"

Everyone shows up, and what was once supposed to be fairly contained gathering turns into every movie about teenagers that has ever been made. That is precisely what happened on my sixteenth birthday.

As people poured in, I started to get super stressed. I figured the best option at that point was to get so drunk that nothing would bother me, and that is exactly what I did. I had a great time, stumbling around like a single-winged social butterfly, until my phone began to vibrate in my pocket. I looked down to get it and saw on the caller ID that it was my home phone calling. I answered with a confused "Hello?" and was not pleased to hear the voice that responded with my name in a stern tone which was that of my mother. She told me to come upstairs and talk to her, so I tried to gather myself and sober up. I took a few deep breaths and then headed inside and upstairs to her office.

When I got there, she immediately yelled, "What the fuck do you think you're doing?" at me. I thought this was a bit much, until I realized that I still had a lit cigarette in my hand. I immediately clenched it in my grasp, burned my palm, and nervously motioned for her to continue. She went on to tell me that I needed to keep the party under control, and that she felt like I took advantage of her by letting this many people come over. I apologized and headed back downstairs.

In the backyard, little to my knowledge, a fight was brewing. Much like any fight amongst teenage boys, there was no good reason for it, and to be honest, I still don't know what the reason for this one was. All I know is that when I got downstairs and went into the backyard, I saw a group of people surrounding a few of my friends, so I rushed in to find out what it was about. As I got into the circle, everyone began to rustle about and in the blink of an eye, it quickly escalated into a brawl. I was trying to stay out of it until I was hit by god-knows-who and then I jumped in like everyone else. I'm sure the whole thing only lasted about thirty to forty-five seconds, and then other partygoers brought it to an end.

Thankfully a close friend of mine, John, who was not involved, kicked the other guys out of my house for me, and the party went on like nothing happened. The rest of the night was kind of a blur, but I remember waking up the next morning and thinking, "Damn, this summer is going to be insane."

The next morning, after the people who crashed at my house cleared out, I had to have the hungover talk with my mother, which I was dreading from the second my eyes opened that morning. She made coffee and we sat in the living room as she explained what a big day of cleaning I had coming, and that she hoped my black eye was worth it. I looked at the backyard and gulped, seeing a wasteland of red cups and cigarette butts. She told me she wanted me to take it easy for the next few days because we were leaving for New York soon, and she didn't want me to be too worn down. I agreed and began the massive cleanup process.

A few days later, my friends John and Zack, along with Matt, met at my house at 4:30am and we all got into my mom's car and headed for the airport. My mother's side of the family has a beach house on Fire Island, which is just off the coast of Long Island, and we go every summer.

This summer, much to my mother's regret, she allowed me to bring three friends, instead of just Matt. Zack and John were my other two friends who I saw everyday. So the five of us headed to LAX to meet my dad at JFK and be on our way.

Once we got there, we all knew we were going to have a fun time. The best way I could possibly describe Fire Island was screen-printed on a t-shirt I once read that said, "Fire Island: A small drinking town with a big fishing problem." That is exactly what this white Anglo-Saxon protestant heaven is. Upon arrival at our beach house we settled into our one big, shared room, went down to the kitchen, and took shots of tequila until we all felt queasy. We went out to the beach and melted in the sun until it was time to go back and have dinner (and more drinks.) We were going to be there for two weeks, so we decided we would also go and spend a few days in New York City, which my parents agreed to.

After a few days at the beach, relaxing with family and taking it easy, we packed up our bags again and headed off to the city. Zack's uncle had an apartment there and was conveniently out of town. He told us we could stay there, and told Zack where he could find a key.

We found ourselves in the heart of the big apple, pockets full of our parent's money, and no plan whatsoever. Lack of plans, I have come to learn, really is at the heart of all evil. They are also at the heart of a lot of the fun I've had, but most of that fun could also be classified as evil. Idle time, no matter how much you crave it as a teenager, really is where all the shit happens. Idle time is the grey area where you either take one path or another.

Our New York trip was that idle time. We partied in the city like we were invincible. We went to bars without getting carded, ate like kings, and roamed the big apple. New York City really is the city that never sleeps… it just passes out.

Each night in New York had a different twist or turn that left us separated. One night, Matt ended up going home with a thirty-year-old lesbian, whose virginity he took. Another night, we completely lost Zack, only to find him sleeping on the subway, as we went to look for him. New York is a dream for some people, but it has always been too much for me. It's fun in doses, but I could not imagine spending more than a year of my life there. We all ran out of money at roughly the same time and headed back to the island to meet my parents.

The whole last week of the trip I felt like something was absent from my life, and on our final night there, I figured out what it was. I had snuck off just before dinner to have a cigarette on the beach, and as I sat in the sand, enjoying the sunset on the ocean, I figured out what it was. It was Taylor. I had trouble pinpointing what felt like it was missing from me, because I was on vacation with my closest friends, and my family, but then it hit me. I may have been with my closest friends, but I realized I wasn't with my best friend. Taylor had somehow snuck into my life like a ninja and became the center of my world. The realization hit me like a train, and as I sat there, finishing my cigarette, I thought of her, and debated the pros and cons of what this realization could do to our current relationship, and what it could maybe turn into.

The whole flight back, and even once I arrived, all I could think about was the haunting realization that had dawned on me. I always thought that when I really fell hard for someone, I would be so happy, but that was not the case. I was just plain upset by the fact that I loved Taylor. I knew that I was going to have to confront this, and I knew it was probably going to go horribly.

Within an hour of touching down in Los Angeles, I got a text from Taylor wanting to hang out, and I stupidly replied something along the lines of "Totally!"

I saw her that night, and it went just as badly as I expected. We had a great time, she was smiling and being cute, and I couldn't take my eyes off of her. I honestly don't think I ever shifted my gaze. All of the things that just seemed "cute" when I first laid eyes on her now shined brighter than the sun. Taylor has these beautiful brown eyes that could turn a rock into liquid. Her smile, hair, demeanor, everything, could be summed up by the word "perfect." If I tried to create my "perfect woman," Taylor would still make her look like the evil inbred twin of two monsters from hell. The only downside was that her new boyfriend was in the apartment just upstairs, and I was obviously not his biggest fan.

When I finally left and went home, I thought about how to approach the subject with her because I knew I needed to say something. I also knew that I just met her asshole of a new boyfriend, and chances were that wasn't going to just vanish upon my request. He was nice enough, too. In any other context this guy and me could be friends, but he had the love of my life, so his title quickly became "Taylor's asshole new boyfriend." I had only met him twice, both times picturing his death as we exchanged pleasantries.

After a few days, I decided that I had to talk to her and feel out these unexplored waters, so I met her at her friend's house and we went outside to talk. I remember so vividly sitting by the pool of this girl's apartment building, in those cheap white beach chairs apartment buildings sometimes have, and nervously chain smoking Marlboro Reds, trying to find the right words.

— "What's up? Is everything okay?" she asked me in a variety of different ways over the next twenty minutes.
— "Yes" I kept assuring her, trying to fight the feeling that I was going to be a coward and walk away from this having said nothing.

Finally, after all the small talk in the world had been gone over at least once, I took a deep breath, and said nothing again. I told her I had to leave and that's exactly what I did. I got in my car and sped off, looking like a total idiot. I don't know how I thought she didn't know what I was doing back then, but looking at it now, I couldn't have been any more obvious.

Over the next few weeks, we still saw each other all the time, and I just forced the thoughts into the back of my head. I was falling for Taylor more and more each day, I guess I thought that maybe if I just fell until I hit the bottom, she might join me there.

We actually grew even closer during this time, and we would jokingly flirt all the time, and have fun around other people who constantly speculated that we had something going on secretly. This drove her boyfriend crazy, but he was leaving for college at the end of the week, and I was banking on that putting enough strain on their relationship to give me a window of opportunity.

That is exactly what happened one eventful night at a girl named Sofie's house, a friend of ours, whose parents were out of town. It was the last weekend before school started, so it wasn't a big group of people, just a few friends hanging out and drinking that night, playing beer pong, etc. Towards the end of the night, when everyone else had calmed down and stopped drinking, Matt and I decided to continue. We both took a few more shots, and then Matt's phone went off. Matt saw that it was his mother calling and hesitantly answered it.

I will never know the tone or fluctuation in his mom's voice as she told him. All I will remember was Matt's face turning pale, and the wave of sadness that crushed over his eyes. He spoke to her for a little bit longer in broken one-word answers and then hung up. He looked at me and said, " 8-Ball is dead." He started tearing up and walked into the backyard, me in pursuit behind him.

He sat down on a bench, speechless, and just started to cry. Matt told me he got shot point blank. As he told me, I started tearing up, as well. I was always surprised by how much 8-Ball's death affected Matt and I. It might have been because he was really the first person we ever knew who had died, and the alcohol in our systems definitely didn't help, but we both broke down. Matt started punching the ground in an upset rage and loudly blurting out obscenities. The girls came outside and tried to comfort Matt, as I remained on the bench, upset and speechless.

As the girls started to calm him down, I walked inside without saying a word to anybody. I climbed into bed in the room that Sofie had told me I could crash in that night. I have never been a flamboyantly emotional person, so I just shed a few tears as I lay on my back, staring at the ceiling. After a few minutes in this room, the door opened and in came Taylor. She asked if I was doing okay and I assured her I would be fine. I told her I wasn't joking around, and that I wasn't trying to make a move on her, but I needed someone to lay down with me for a little, and she got right into bed.

I thanked her for this as we lay there, staring at the ceiling. I was about to apologize to her for being weird over the last few weeks when she completely surprised me by rolling on top of me and beginning to kiss me.

Even though this came at a moment when it was the last thing on my mind, I had been waiting for that kiss for an entire summer, and it completely halted my sadness with a rush of pure joy. I thought I would never have a better night with anyone in my whole life. I didn't get laid; all we did was kiss, but it was still the best night I've ever had with anyone. It was one of those romantic comedy nights. Kisses were interrupted by smiles and inside jokes until I don't even remember passing out.

I arose the next morning feeling like a new man. I woke up just before Taylor, and I rolled over to see her back, cementing into my head that the whole night wasn't a dream from which I would awake disappointed. After the smile wore off my face, sitting there in bed, the skull-crushing hangover began to set in, and I immediately lay back down.

Taylor still wasn't up yet, so I snuck out of the room, into the back yard and lit a cigarette, quenching my thirst with what was left of a bottle of orange juice that someone was using as a chaser. Matt, who looked like he got hit by a train, came outside and joined me. He sat down, without saying a word, and I handed him the cigarette. He took a few drags and handed it back. I told him what happened with Taylor, and he finally perked up a little. I told him all of the details, like teenage boys do, and he responded with an approving high-five. He knew how badly I wanted Taylor, and when it comes to best friends, accomplishments like that mean almost as much to both of you.

As happy as he may have been for me, he made sure to give me fair warning about the possible repercussions of my actions. He was always against relationships. He said there was just no point.

Chances are that you're not going to end up with the person, so why wait until you inevitably get hurt, time and time again. He never needed anyone specific. I, on the other hand, have always loved the idea. I can clearly see the downside, though, but let's be honest — it's nice to wake up next to someone. It's often even better than falling asleep next to them. That's an important thing to remember, though it's often forgot.

The girls eventually joined us in the back, but with everyone around, Taylor and I didn't really acknowledge what happened the night before. We all hung out, trying to recover until Matt and I left, both going back to our respective homes. We started school the next day, and much to our dismay, we had to get at least a little prepared.

I waited a few days to see if Taylor would bring it up first, but when she didn't, I took it into my own hands. She was acting weird towards me since it happened, and I think that was mainly because neither of us really knew what to do. I finally decided we needed to talk about it, so I called her. I asked her what she thought about that night, and she said she had wanted to ask me the same thing.

I told her that I asked first so she had to start, and she reluctantly began what I assumed is a speech she had been going over in her head for days. She told me that we were too close to just casually hook up, and that having just got out of the relationship she was in, she did not want to jump back into another.

This is not what I wanted to hear. I spent some time trying to convince her otherwise, but eventually I came to terms with the fact that we were on different pages. I told her how perfect I thought we'd be, but it didn't change a thing. I told her that I needed to clear my head for a week or so and then everything would go back to normal. I hung up after that.

The next day at school, Taylor was sitting in front of me in our computer class, and at one point I noticed that she was crying. I messaged her computer saying that I did not take back anything I said the night before, but that I apologized if any of it made her cry. She turned around and asked me if I would go outside and talk to her, which I agreed to and we left the room.

We sat on a bench in the back of the school, and Taylor told me between tears that she couldn't picture a day without me. She said she wanted to try "us" out if it meant not losing me. I told her to only say it if she really meant it, and that she wasn't saving me from anything, but she persisted. Looking into her eyes I believed what she was saying and I kissed her again, for the second time in my life. It's funny that to this day I can remember every kiss, and they all haunt me like a dark cloud that follows me everywhere I go.

For the next few weeks, Taylor and I did everything together. I'd steal kisses at school, we would go to dinner and movies, it was exactly what I had always wanted. I really can't, to this day, think of a time in my life that I was happier.

This all of course came to a screeching halt soon after. One night at Matt's house, Taylor and Sofie came over for a little while and Taylor seemed very strange. When they were leaving, I walked them out to their car. I went to kiss Taylor goodbye and she turned her head, letting my lips land on her cheek. She said she didn't like kissing with lip-gloss on, and the red flags popped up all over. I somehow managed to smile and say goodnight, but I knew then and there that this was the beginning of the end.

I waited until the next day at school to talk to her about it. I tried to bring it up casually, but I'm pretty sure it came out desperate. My subtext wasn't screaming "What? Why? Please no!" in a pathetic attempt to change fate. She took a breath and told me that she only said she wanted to be with me to make me happy. She said she tried to force herself to have the feelings, but there was just nothing there. Each word landed like a punch from Mike Tyson. I swallowed the explosive word vomit that was trying to find its way out of my mouth. I just nodded for the remainder of her little speech and then just got up and walked away. I got in my car and left school early, driving straight home.

This was the first time in my life that I felt completely helpless. I knew that no matter what I did, I could not change how someone felt. There was nothing I could do. I defaulted to just collapsing in bed and taking a nap.

When I woke up, I arose a different man. I felt like I had gained twenty pounds. A weight that collected it's mass in a jumble of knowledge, pain, and reality. This heaviness went everywhere with me after that. I went to school, and kept my schedule the exact same, but I didn't smile once.

Taylor and I would see each other around and just ignore each other. I knew she felt bad, but I didn't care. I wasn't going to give her the satisfaction of my understanding. I was sleeping all the time, and when I wasn't, I was drinking. I wasn't doing it socially, and no one knew I was drunk, but I was guzzling whiskey like it was Gatorade after a big game.

One day, my dad came into my room and said, "C'mon, get up, we're going out." This is the last thing that I wanted to do, but he made it pretty clear in his tone of voice that it was not a request, or an invitation, this was a demand. We went to a coffee shop and sat down. Just to be the thorn in his side, I lit a cigarette right in front of him. This was the first cigarette he ever saw me smoke, and looking back now, I think about how dumb I must have looked.

He asked me what was going on, and after a barrage of other questions, I finally just told him the whole story. When I was done he asked me, "What's the deal with her mom?" This caught me off guard.

— "What do you mean? Like is she in the picture? She lives with her for half the week." I told him.
— "So they're divorced?" He asked me, even though I made that pretty obvious already.
—"Yes." I declared again, this time more deadpan, trying to make sure he heard me.
— "Well that could explain a lot of what's going on, at least for her. I'm not saying it would change anything, but understanding where someone comes from in the sense of the relationship models they have seen, can often make their actions more understandable."

He was very understanding. He knew growing up was hard, and he sympathized with what I was going through. He told me about his first heartbreak, and how hard it was for him, but like the sixteen-year-old I was, I could not get it through my thick skull that anyone else could have possibly ever felt how I was feeling. He told me what a milestone this was in my life, and that it really was a blessing in disguise. He then went on to give me the best advice I have every gotten to this day.

"When you come to a fork in the road, you have to go one way or the other. You can make yourself a victim to everyone else, or you can stand up and take it all in stride. As a man, you need to learn how to be a warrior. You need to learn how to fight for yourself, and know that your most valuable tool, asset, and friend is yourself. If you just collapse into depression, she wins, Buddy. You need to move on, keep your focus straight ahead of you, and make it your goal to be her biggest regret."

I know he didn't mean any of that in the vindictive way that I took it and used it. But those words still to this day, even though they have changed meaning a bit, ring as loud as a million bells. I told him I was going to come out of this stronger than ever, and I think he saw in my eyes that his words really landed and made an impact, because after that we got in the car and drove home.

The next day in school, my English teacher told us about our newest assignment. We were told to write a letter to ourselves five years in the future, and that in five years, he would send us that letter.

I thought this was an awesome assignment, but I knew that, unfortunately, my English teacher was a huge asshole and the possibility of him actually sending these back out to us in five years was very, very small.

I still used it as an opportunity to vent my Taylor problems, and enclosed in the envelope the only picture I had of us kissing, and a four-page letter asking myself if I ever got her back. I knew that Taylor was the love of my life, and even though it made me miserable, I was praying that in five years she would still be torturing me at the very least.

About a week after that assignment, the teacher had some big blowout with my school's board of trustees, or someone high up, because I never saw him again. This was probably for the best because he wasn't that great of a teacher, but I hated the fact that in his possession was a letter that I desperately wanted to read again at some point in my life.

I couldn't wait for seventeen to get here. I was finally on the other end of my slump, or so I thought, and I made a vow to myself to change my life up a bit. The Taylor experience really jumbled up everything I knew, and instead of straightening out what was already in my head, I decide to reorganize and become someone I had never been before. Of course I knew that deep down I was who I was, and I couldn't change that, but people grow into themselves based off the decisions they make, and I was going to start making different choices.

Up until this point in my life, even though I would party, and do things that some may equate to the life of a "bad kid," I was actually quite nice. I was a prime choice for a beautiful girl to friend zone, and throughout my teenage years, this happened more and more. Sex was easy, random hook-ups, or drunken party kisses, but whenever I actually had feelings for anyone, they were never reciprocated. This was most recently demonstrated by Taylor's monstrous blow to my subconscious. I was sick and tired of hearing that "We're too close," or that someone who I saw something in "didn't want to lose me as a friend."

I've always thought those cop out excuses were funny. No matter what you say, in any relationship, when one person develops feelings for the other, anything that has happened up until that point is dead and gone. The dawning reality of the chemical mix up in the victim's head make it so that there is only one direction to go, and only one path to get there. By saying that "I don't want to lose you as a friend," you are effectively signing your friendship's death warrant.

I was tired of being that sucker, and in this, my seventeenth year on this planet, I decided I was going to learn how to be an asshole. When you have always been the sweet, caring, kind of guy this seems like a difficult task, but it really isn't. It's so hard to imagine being one of those guys that just don't care, but when you actually try, you can catch on fairly quickly. It may not be morally satisfying, or rewarding in any way, but it sure is fun. I was young, but I felt like I was old enough to leave my ideas of love behind me. Besides, I was in my final year of high school, a year some people look back on in golden light, while others bury it deep in a hole only a well-trained therapist can unearth. I optimistically thought I would be one of the golden-lighters' and wanted to reap all the benefits possible.

It was fun. Honest, good-hearted, heavily intoxicated fun. I might have been partying too much for my age, or really for any age, but the rest of my life actually seemed to start falling into place. My grades were good, my college applications were sent in. The asshole thing was working out really well for me. Even though the people who really knew me, knew it was an act, everyone else was pretty easily fooled. I was having better luck with girls than I had ever had, and it made me feel wanted and loved. None of it actually mattered, or meant anything at all, but I was trying to prove a point to myself, the world, and especially Taylor.

Taylor and I had just started talking again, but the words exchanged were much more that of acquaintances, as opposed to the friends we were. This was in part due to the fact that even though I wouldn't admit it, I was still in love with Taylor, and everything I did, as much as I believed it was for me, was for her to see. I made it a point to flirt with her friends, befriend people she knew, and make sure that wherever she went, she would hear about me. Much like a ghost or a monster, when she stopped believing in me as part of her reality, I tried to haunt her dreams.

Los Angeles, as I've mentioned, just got more toxic as I grew older. It seemed like every day, new opportunities were opening up for me, and these were not opportunities in the sense of jobs, or anything like that. The house parties turned into nightclubs, the dance parties turned into raves, and before I knew it, every weekend, I was intoxicated in some way or another. This, as scary as it sounds, was actually the reality for most of the senior class at my high school. The parties got better, but we were also getting smarter, growing older, and we wore the camouflage of acceptance letters and grades, so parents went on smiling, believing their child was an angel.

I am a product of a generation that threw old stereotypes to the wind. The stoner, in most cases, was no longer the tie-dye shirt wearing, dread lock sporting waste, as pictured in 70's rock 'n' roll movies like Sean Penn's Spicoli. The stoner was a lot more hidden, and a lot more productive than previously assumed by the generations' preceding mine. I grew up with straight A students, well-spoken kids, who drank, smoked, and snorted everything under the sun. I would run into our valedictorian at raves. This made the warning signs a lot blurrier, and in most cases, non-existent to parents.

I knew that I needed to get it together this year, so I applied to great schools, and decided that I wanted to pursue a degree in the film industry. I was never able to imagine myself in a suit, working a nine to five job, so my top school choices were New York University, University of Southern California, and University of Texas, all schools with great film programs.

When the acceptance letters rolled in, I was horribly disappointed. I got into none of my top three choices, and was only wait-listed at my number four, California State University Long Beach. I knew they had a good film program, and that it is where Spielberg went, so I put the remainder of my hopes in that basket and continued on with my year. Luckily, a few weeks later, I received my official acceptance from CSULB, and had the weight of my future temporarily lifted off my shoulders.

I remember how proud my parents were of my going to college, and they made sure, as parents do, to inform every one of their friends and relatives. Every one I knew was getting into schools left and right as well, so parties quickly became overwhelmed with sayings like "hey man, congrats" or "you're going to be great there." Even with how common hearing these phrases became, I was still taken back and grateful when I heard them muttered to me by Taylor. I ran into her at a party, and it was the first time in a while that we said anything of any importance to each other.

We went outside to smoke a cigarette, and thus began a pattern in our relationship that we would never break. We sat out front of the house, away from the mayhem, and talked about how we were. We talked about us, talked about what happened between us, and said our separate apologies. Somewhere in the middle of her speech about how proud she was of me, yet how she knew the person I had become recently wasn't really me, we became best friends again. The thing about Taylor and I, the thing that always drove me back, was that we were virtually the same person. We got along so well because it was like we shared a brain. Things that no one else would laugh at would have Taylor and I rolling on the floor. We understood each other completely, and I think that's why it was always so hard, even impossible, for me to completely walk away.

As it would turn out, we both ended up having the same fatal flaw. Neither of us could ever let ourselves be happy. At least I can speak for myself, and I need the deep end. I need to be close to the edge. Taylor, on the other hand, didn't need anybody. I refused to be content and she refused to dependent. This is why we spent years and years of our lives crashing into each other. One of us could never let the other get too close, or too far away.

We tried to ease back into our friendship slowly, but with two people like us, that's never as easy as it sounds. We were right back to spending every minute with each other, but unfortunately, my feelings for her never changed. As great as it was being back in a good place with her, I still died inside every time she talked about a guy or did something cute. I eventually got better at hiding it, and for a while, I think I actually had her fooled into thinking I was over those silly feelings I once had.

I began dating a girl named Chloe who had just recently broken up with her boyfriend. I had seen her around school before, and always thought she was cute, but the day after her relationship ended, she walked into the class we shared looking like she was ready for a photo shoot. After I picked my jaw up off the floor, I made it my goal to get to know this girl, and I did. After a week or two of being not nearly as smooth as I thought I was, I got her number and we made plans to hang out.

The first time I hung out with Chloe outside of school we ended up getting way too drunk, and having sex. This is exactly what I wanted on paper, but the reality of how easy this seemingly difficult task was came as a huge shock to me. The next day we spent the whole day together, and it turned out she was actually a really cool girl. When I left the next night I kissed her, and for some reason blurted out the words "Hey, don't fuck anyone else, okay?" This seemed to be the old me shining through the asshole I was trying to become, because I saw how the words landed, and she smiled.

For the next few weeks, we were completely wrapped up in our own world. My friends, family, and life became background to this reality we created for ourselves. This arrangement was interpreted differently by both of us, and that quickly, and unfortunately, became evident to me. I was so used to being the one that fell, I was so self-consumed that I didn't notice her tumbling down hill. At first, I so wanted this girl that I thought was so great to be interested in me, that I totally disregarded the fact that maybe she was. I was so used to being the victim, that I didn't realize I might actually be the victimizer.

The night I realized how much Chloe liked me I thought it was wonderful. I agreed with everything she said, and totally mislead her. It wasn't on purpose, and I really did think I felt the same way she did until I got away for a little and really thought about it. When I put all my cards on the table, and really looked at what was there, I realized I didn't like Chloe at all, I just liked someone liking me. Feeling needed and wanted was so important to me, and had been absent from my life for so long that I pounced on the opportunity without realizing that there is almost always another side to it.

Things between Chloe and I got really weird after that, and while she grew more and more fond of me, I started to pinpoint every one of her idiosyncrasies and faults, and quickly built mountains out of mole hills. By the end of the next few weeks, every word that came out of her mouth was like nails on a chalkboard to me. The only reason I was still talking to her really was because of the sex and the idea of me being with someone began to get under Taylor's skin a little bit. She never mentioned it, or brought it up, but subtext sometimes speaks louder than words.

She would get passive aggressive anytime Chloe's name would get brought up. When I was with her, and Chloe was present or even talked about she would get fidgety, like her opinion was trying to get out of her mouth and she was fighting to keep it in.

Much to my dismay, I took my self-appointed role as an asshole to heart, and ended up treating her horribly. One night while my parents were out of town a few friends came over, and I ended up sleeping with one of Chloe's "close friends." The fact that she would sleep with me is a pretty strong indicator that she wasn't a great friend to Chloe, but that still didn't excuse my actions.

I felt horrible the next day and told Chloe everything that happened. She wasn't nearly as mad as I thought she would be. She was almost understanding, and even though the possibility of a relationship between us was gone, she almost felt bad for me. She told me that I "needed to figure my shit out before I would ever be happy with someone" and then left. She got into her car and left me sitting at a coffee shop, cigarette still in my mouth, pondering the words she said over and over again in my own head.

My predilection towards love, and my ideas of happiness had finally come back to bite me in the ass. I felt horrible. This whole "asshole" thing that I thought I wanted so badly was not nearly as rewarding as I hoped it would be. As much as I have always been predisposed to revenge, and constantly victimizing myself to achieve a sad drunken means to an end, hurting someone else was not nearly what I thought it would be like. Not caring at all was fun at first, but I knew I had to find a happy medium. The old me got hurt, and the new me hurt people, so maybe, somewhere in the middle, existed some sort of a silver lining.

School finished up pretty quickly. The beginning of the year seemed to take so long, but that last month or two flew by so fast. Before I knew it graduation was over and I was officially on summer break. Life was actually really looking up. Taylor and I were right back to our old selves, my summer was shaping up to be pretty promising, and I was about to officially be an adult.

Finally eighteen. This was a time I had been waiting for since I was old enough to really appreciate the freedom that the future held. I didn't feel like any more of a man than I had just a few weeks before, but I did all the cliché stuff like buy my first legal pack of cigarettes, and a lotto ticket, etc. I unfortunately did not win the lottery, but it felt pretty damn close sitting in my backyard drinking beers with my closest friends and family.

An array of friends and acquaintances stopped by throughout the day, some staying all day, others just for a few minutes. By the time night rolled around I was nice and drunk, and the only people that were still there were my parents and my friend John. John and I were trying to figure out what to do until I was invited by some girls I knew to join them at a strip club. While at first we laughed at the idea, I realized out of all the crazy shit I had done, somehow I had skipped that shameful, needed step in becoming a man. When I brought this up to John he said he actually hadn't been to one either and we got in the car.

I remember walking in and being a little disappointed. For some reason until you set foot in a strip club you imagine this golden palace full of perfect bodies and sexy smiles, but that is not at all what it is like. It's extremely dark, and as we found the stage the girls I knew were sitting at, I looked at the stack of one dollar bills in my hand and could just picture myself at forty years old, in a stained wife beater, masturbating to internet porn that my wife knew nothing about. It was not a pretty sight.

The room was quickly illuminated when a dancer by the name of Mackenzie set foot on the stage. I swear that to this day, in all honesty, Mackenzie was the most beautiful girl I had ever seen in my life. I threw almost all my money on that stage.

I looked at John after she left the stage, and he seemed to be in just about the same awe that I was in. I watched the next few dancers, tossing the rest of my money half-heartedly until I felt a hand on my shoulder.

— "Are you guys going to buy him a dance?" said the voice behind me. I turn around and see Mackenzie talking to the girls that I was with.
— "We're out of money" one of the girls responds. I looked at the wall and saw that private dances were sixty-five dollars, money I had already unfortunately spent.
— "I'm out too." I tell her.
— "It's your birthday, right?" she asks to my surprise. I tell her that it is and she simply replies "well then happy birthday."

She grabs me by the hand, and guides me to the back of the club into a private room and she sat me down on a chair, closing the curtain behind her. We talked for a good ten minutes or so before she started to dance. She seemed to really like me. An act all strippers have, I presumed, but then it continued. She asked me questions about my life, and I could hear the lies just pouring out of me. I was twenty-one. I was a writer. My agency was CAA. I lived in Hollywood. All of these things not true. I wanted to impress her so badly.

When she finally started giving me a lap dance, something that I still think is awkward to this day, she started to kiss me. I was torn. This girl, gorgeous beyond words, seemed so interested in me, but she was a stripper. At first I tried to fight any urge I had, but as I got lost in the few minutes I had with her, I got more and more into it. As soon as I finally manned up and decided to take some initiative, she stopped me. She pointed to a sign above me that read, "No Touching." I was so confused. She was just all over me, literally, but I wasn't allowed to do anything? She went right back into the dance but the illusion was shattered. The song ended and I could hear my name being called from the main room. I gave her a small tip out of the money I had left and exited the club.

The next morning came with an incurable hangover, and child-like thoughts of what Mackenzie and I's life would have been like. I got lunch with Taylor, in an attempt to get something else in my system besides alcohol. We met at a diner near my house and she handed me a little envelope with "Happy Birthday" written across the front of it. I said I would open it later and we went on with our lunch. I asked her why she wasn't at my party the day before and she gave me the last answer I wanted to hear. She said she was with her new boyfriend, and she apologized for blowing me off. Even though I wish she hadn't, she then went on to tell me about her new boyfriend, Chris.

She had been seeing Chris off and on for a few months now, and he continued to keep her in a state of perpetual confusion. While he had her believing that he may see a future there, I knew if he didn't already, he never would. I tried to explain this to her, but she didn't listen. I knew first hand because I just got done doing this with Chloe. I decided to change the subject before we just broke into another argument.

Taylor had horrible taste in men, at least in my opinion, so I had to pick and choose my battles while talking about them. She loved these assholes with no potential, which always perplexed me, but so did most of the girls I knew. There's something about someone who doesn't care that makes people feel they need to change or fix these people. They don't. But all I can do is observe, because if there is something I was beginning to wrap my head around, it was that you couldn't change people. No one.

The rest of the summer went by very joyously. I was going out with friends, having fun and getting a clearer and clearer view of what I wanted to do with my life. I was still seeing Taylor almost every day, which was great, but her grip on me had not loosened whatsoever. I had come to terms with the feelings I had, and gotten better at suppressing them. I just kept the belief in the back of my head that one day she would come to her senses and see in us, what I saw in us. It also helped that I was occupied with short flings and romances with an array of girls who actually saw potential in me.

When it was finally time for me to go off to college, I realized I wanted to stay at home forever. Leaving the nest is a weird experience no matter how long you've dreamed of it. I remember the drive with my parents to see my jail cell, or dorm, as they called it, for the first time. I knew right then that school was not for me.

When they finally left, I spent the night sitting in my dorm with a bottle of Captain Morgan, staring at all of my belongings packed up into cardboard boxes. I have never been so unenthused by anything in my life.

As school started I began to get into the groove of things a little better. I made some friends, most of whom I met in the Designated Smoking Area, or DSA, of the dorm buildings. I started to enjoy myself more and more as the days went by, and before I knew it, I had my own little social circle.

If you allow yourself to accept college for what it is, it really proves that all the movies and television shows are accurate. I was not one for the Greek system, or the clubs, so it was a little harder for me to find my groove at school, but finally I did, as everyone eventually does. The parties and nightlife at college are totally different than anywhere else in the world. College is a mix of geniuses, idiots, kids who partied all through high school, and kids who had never partied before in their lives. This varied collection in the demographic of these crowded living rooms and backyards lead to a clash of people that all inevitably get black out drunk together.

I was not one of the "had never partied before" kids, but I still used higher education as an excuse to perpetuate my substance abuse even further. By the time I was in the middle of my first semester I was going out almost every night. I was drinking more than I had ever drank, going to class hungover, and then repeating the cycle seven days a week. It was just so fun. These parties had no rules, no one had any curfews, and hormones filled the air like a poisonous gas.

Having sex in college is about as hard as a cloud. People just go nuts. You would get to a party, lose total inhibition, begin speaking with someone, and before you knew it you would be ripping their shirt off in your dorm room, hoping your roommate didn't walk in. There's nothing special, or meaningful about it, which at the time is fine, but I began to get numb to it. I realized that I had slept with almost twenty women since I had lost my virginity, but I had never "made love." I always thought this was just a term parents used for any carnal acts, but it's more than that. You don't realize the difference until you've had one and not the other. I knew I wanted something more in my life, but I was having too much fun to do anything about it.

The drug culture amongst young adults varies from place to place, each group worried about their own generation, but I was really getting worried about my peers. Weed and prescription pills were big amongst my high school and early-teen peers, but once I was away at school, the recreational use of everything seemed to be widely accepted. There is a shocking lack of lethargy and/or schizophrenia at college campuses in comparison to the amount of drugs that are consumed. Given my almost total lack of will, I tried everything offered to me. I was not one for pills, or downers really, but cocaine really kept my boat afloat. The first time I did a line was in a friend's dorm room before we went out that night, and about an hour afterwards I decided that was the drug for me.

When that night was over, I had a splitting hangover, and only bits and pieces of memory that I could recall. I looked at myself in the mirror, and was almost taken back at my own reflection. The "freshman fifteen" usually means a freshman gains fifteen pounds when he/she starts school, but that was not the case this particular morning. I could see my ribs poking out, and I came to terms that my diet of whiskey, rum, and nicotine needed to end soon. That day I made the first of many resolutions I would say and not keep; I was going to calm down, get it together, and focus on school.

This worked for a few weeks, and by the time winter break came around, I arrived back home with a healthy smile, and a normal number on the scale. This thrilled my parents, who were expecting the worst. The 3.6 GPA that I had achieved up to by the time I came home also pleasantly surprised them. Needless to say, I was expecting winter break to be a calm, nice, walk in the park.

As I usually am, I was wrong. When school finally got out for break I drove back to my parents house, where I would be staying for the next five weeks. The first person I saw aside from Matt was Taylor. Taylor got me excited when she told me how she had ended things with Chris finally, and then immediately brought me back down when she started telling me about some new guy she had been seeing, and how happy she was. I feigned a smile, and lied about how happy I was for her. I was happy to see her, though. That much was true, so I gritted my teeth, and clenched through the rest of her incoherent speech about learning to respect herself.

Since everyone I had gone to high school with pretty much were all getting back into town around the same time, there was a lot of catching up with people, which was nice. The parties were nothing like that of our high school years just a short time ago. A few beers, no more than ten or fifteen people, it was all very calm.

One night, at my friend Sarah's house, I ran into a girl that I only barely knew in school named Shelby. Shelby and I got to talking that night, and even though I had sworn I wasn't going to get involved with anyone for a while, I asked her to get dinner with me that weekend. She said she would love to.

We went out and had a great time. I was really surprised with how similar we were, that we weren't closer in high school. It was probably because I come off so unapproachable, or as she would later put it "I just kind of looked like an asshole."

We started hanging out almost every day, dates here and there, a winter fling if you will. Zack's birthday was coming up in a few days, and he had rented a cabin for him and his friends. Zack was bringing his girlfriend Dora, and John was also bringing a lady-friend, so I thought I would go out on a limb and invite Shelby to join us on the trip.

Shelby was thrilled to be invited, and we all headed up the next morning. The drive up was really nice, and when we got there, I spent almost the whole day with Shelby sitting on the big balcony, bundled in sweaters, sipping gin and tonics while staring at the beautiful wilderness through slowly doubling vision. We were there for four days and three nights, a quick getaway, but we all did our best to make the most of it. The days consisted of hiking/stumbling around the woods, finding trails, drinking and exploring. We would all cook dinner every night, and then continue the party inside the cabin. Everyone had their own bedrooms, and sleeping with Shelby every night like that actually made me feel really comfortable. After trying to fight off having real feelings for anyone for so long, I could actually feel myself falling for this girl.

On our last night there, I went out onto the balcony alone to have a cigarette. There was a nice rocking chair out there and I just sat by myself for the first time on the trip. Everybody else was downstairs watching a movie or in their rooms. As I took my last drag and put my cigarette out, Zack's little brother came out to join me. Zack's brother, Gregory, was just finally old enough to hang out with us, and though he kept to himself most of the trip, he proved to be a huge part of my trip.

He sat down next to me and said, "I think Matt is trying to get with Shelby." This grabbed my attention initially, but knowing Matt for almost five years now, I told him it probably wasn't the case.

"I'm pretty sure what I saw, Bro" he said. I continued to rebut his comments, but they started to land, and I got angrier and angrier. Finally I decided to go downstairs and check for myself. As I made my way to the stairs, Matt was struggling up them. I pulled him to the side. I asked him if he tried to, or did, hook up with Shelby, and he exclaimed, "no way, Man!" Matt was beyond drunk, so I left it at that. Later that night, I got into bed with Shelby, trying not to say anything dumb or accusatory, and instead of bringing it up again, I decided to make her mine, regardless. This was the first, and last, night we ever had sex. It went from drunk and sloppy, to passionate and aggressive in a matter of seconds. I don't remember when or how I fell asleep that night, but I woke up a few hours later, at the crack of dawn, before anyone else in the house.

The worry of Matt and Shelby had not shaken from me as I showered and made myself some coffee. I enjoyed the sunrise by myself, hoping nothing from last night was true. Everybody finally got up around the same time, and we cleaned up the cabin and made some breakfast. We had to be out by noon that day. After breakfast I pulled Matt to the side again, now sober, and asked him about the Shelby situation. He was still adamant that nothing happened. Matt reassured me over and over again, until my questioning finally ceased. I still had a weird lingering feeling, but I left it alone. The drive back was quiet, seeing as Shelby and I were both horribly hungover. I could also tell she felt weird about something, possibly our sex, because she had always said "I'm the kind of girl you have to wait for."

I dropped her off and went home. I planned on napping for at least a few hours, exhausted from the last few days, and within minutes of arriving back at my parent's house, that is exactly what I did. I dreamt of Matt and Shelby while I napped, snapping me awake in a horrible mood a few hours later. When I checked my phone I saw that I had a text from Matt.

Matt's apology for having hooked up with Shelby was long and pathetic, continually referencing his own cowardice. It didn't matter to me though. I went cold. It wasn't about the action as much as it was that a close friend could look me in the eye and lie... twice. And Shelby, she fucked me just a few minutes after. I threw my phone across the room, shattering it on the opposite wall. I had never felt more betrayed.

The next few days consisted of apology attempts from both parties, all immediately shut down by me. I told them I wasn't mad, I just didn't want anything to do with them. What really bothered me was that I let my guard down again, and boom, I was immediately attacked by reality. First Taylor, now Shelby, I was quickly hardening to the idea of happily-ever-after. My pre-existing, childish thoughts of love were dying at a rapid pace, and while it may have been less fulfilling, I've never shed a tear after a random hook-up or one-night stand.

I was more disillusioned than ever when I finally went back to school, and decided to finish the semester up with flying colors. I was still partying, but I made sure school came first this time. I needed something to occupy my mind, and I figured what the hell, why not let that be my education. Both Matt and Shelby had tried contacting me a few times, one blaming the other, or vice versa, but I didn't care. I was slowly learning that the only person who was going to watch after or care for me was myself. I didn't need anyone in my life that I couldn't trust.

The only people I still talked to at home really were Taylor and John. John and I would just shoot the shit occasionally, and Taylor would call me here and there. Taylor would complain about her guy problems, and how none of them cared about her. I would play along, making up embellished stories of my own love life as I went along. Taylor's self-loathing rants were some of the most frustrating things in the world to hear. This was mainly because the guys she was falling for were the antithesis of what she said she wanted. Funny enough, when she would say what she wanted in a guy, it was like she was reading off my resume, but no, that never clicked for her.

The school year finished up well, and I ended up with straight A's for the first time in my life. I was really involved in my film classes, and finally found what I had some passion for. I loved writing. I liked directing, and some of the producing stuff, but I was really excelling in the screenwriting portion of my classes. I think it is probably because by this point in my life I had dealt with so much shit, my situational canon was full to the brim, and I was tossing a little this or a little that into each story that came my way.

My nineteenth year on this planet could easily be summed up by an array of long drunken fights/talks with Taylor; with a splash of another great girl I let slip through my fingers because I was a huge idiot. School was out and I finally had the much awaited summer break after my first year at college. After living on my own, even if it was a dorm, moving back in with my parents for an elongated period of time wasn't easy. My parents are in no way "hard" to live with, but it's nice to have your own space.

The beginning of the summer was really nice. I caught up on a lot of missed sleep from finals week. Everyone was home again from their schools, travelling, and we all hung out together. I was turning nineteen in a few days, but had no plans whatsoever. I found out that my friend Sarah was throwing me a birthday party, and while the surprise was now gone, I couldn't have been happier.

The party was a lot of fun. It felt like everyone I had ever been friends or even acquaintances with was there. Matt was initially not invited, but I wanted to get petty childhood drama out of my life now that I was getting older, so a few days before the party we sat down and talked. He gave me a great apology, and I told him how much it really hurt, being lied to like that. We settled our differences, and Matt actually ended up DJ'ing the party.

I had started celebrating around noon that day, so by the time the party was really going, around ten or eleven, I was ready to pass out. I was actually starting to just try and find corners in the house that weren't crowded to rest when I heard "T!" yelled from across the room. I turned around to see Christine, the only girl I knew that called me that, coming towards me, her friend in tow.

— "Happy birthday, Thomas!" she said as she approached me, throwing her arms around me in an overly affectionate, girly, drunken embrace. "This is my friend, Megan." she tells me as she pushes her friend in front of her, like a parent introducing their child to a friend from work.
— "It's nice to meet you," I say. Megan was very cute. She was blonde, with big, beautiful, brown eyes. We engaged in some small talk as Christine somehow slowly slipped away. Her plan to pawn off her friend apparently worked, because two hours later, Megan and I had not broken from that conversation.

I was drunk, so I don't remember how we exactly got to the front of the house, but before I knew it, I was kissing Megan up against the wall surrounding the house. And then just like that, a cab pulled up and she left.

The next morning, while recovering from the party, I found a number written on my hand. There was no name to go along with it, but I was pretty sure it was Megan's. I wrote it down on a piece of paper and put it on my desk, planning to call her later that day. I didn't leave the house at all that day because I had to pack for New York the next morning. It was vacation time with the family, and I was meeting them at the beach house the next day. The simple task of packing a bag can be a whole daylong venture when you had the hangover that I did. I completed the packing and took a four-hour nap.

When I awoke, I managed to get out of the house and get some soup at a deli around the corner from my house. I got it to go and ate it in my living room with a handful of Tylenols. While having my post-meal cigarette I had become so accustomed to, I took out Megan's phone number and gave her a call. After a few rings, a soft voice connected on the other side of the call. "Hello?" she asked.

"Hey!" I said, beginning the awkward "it's me from the other night" conversation that sometimes comes along with dating. "Your number was written on me this morning." We talked for a while, and before I knew it, we had been on the phone for almost an hour. I told her I had to go finally, trying to remove myself before I ran out of things to say. I told her I would call her from New York, and she said she couldn't wait to hear from me.

A few days into my vacation, I was sitting up on the outside patio of the beach house, and decided it was the right time to call her. After that night, we spoke every night for the rest of my trip. Her voice had slowly, and surprisingly, become part of my daily schedule. I couldn't wait to get back to California, and Megan.

As soon as I touched down in Los Angeles, I drove right to her apartment. We got some coffee, and went through the awkward transition from phone voices to face-to-face conversation. I really enjoyed Megan's company. We had our first real date a few nights later, and before I knew it, we were spending every day together.

I had never been in a real relationship until now, and seemingly without any hesitation, Megan and I were boyfriend and girlfriend. We would go everywhere together. Everybody told us how cute we were like any new couple. Everyone was very happy for us. Except for Taylor. It really bothered Taylor, which was only an added bonus really. I finally felt like someone cared about me, and while I was worried that she might be a little more invested than I was in the relationship, I just chalked that up to me being a pessimistic, stubborn ass and pushed it to the back of my head.

One night, I can't remember why, but I ended up going out to a party alone. I said I wouldn't drink much, which, like almost every time that is said by anyone, ended up being a lie. I saw some old friends at the party, and after being coaxed into six or seven different "take a shot with me's!" I was sufficiently drunk. My inebriation landed me up on the roof of the apartment building with who else other than my Achilles heel, Taylor.

The conversation started much like any of them do, with just a friendly cigarette. It continued into discussing our relationships. Taylor told me that she didn't think Megan and I were right for each other. This didn't surprise me in the slightest. I listened to the rest of her rant though.

She went on to say some things that actually caught me off guard. She told me that she didn't think we were right for each other because I didn't look at Megan the way that I used to/still look at her. She said she thought I was just in a relationship to be in one. This was something that I had already feared myself, but I stuck to my guns and told her she was wrong between dry gulps and the beginning of a nervous sweat. She knew me so damn well.

When I finally got the conversation to shift to her issues, she went on to talk about another one of the numerous guys who didn't really like her. She was so upset. She didn't understand why no one she was interested in wanted to be with her. I told her in a half–joking, half brutally honest smirk that I think she had a total misunderstanding of the saying "fuck anything that doesn't make you happy." She almost slapped me.

She was more upset than I had ever really seen her. She felt so un-cared for. She said that she didn't think anyone would ever love her. I couldn't stand to hear this, so I did something I would wind up regretting for the rest of my life. I couldn't listen to her bitch that no one cared about her to the one person in the world who cared for her more than anything, so I told her that when she and I broke up I tried to kill myself. This was not true, but that didn't stop me from divulging farther and farther into this lie that I couldn't ever come back from. I told her that I had a gun in my mouth and couldn't pull the trigger because I didn't want to hurt her. As these words flowed from my mouth all I could think was "what the fuck are you doing?!" I had a girlfriend. I was making up a horrible lie, but I couldn't stop. Taylor started crying, pulling me into her, while also punching me in the chest.

— "What is wrong with you?!" she managed to get out between tears.
— "So much you don't even know," I told her.

I just wanted her to know how much she could mean to someone. I went about it the wrong way, but I think I got the message across, because the rest of the night was the sweetest Taylor had been to me in years. The

Taylor I had fallen in love with. The Taylor with whom, whether I liked it or not, I was still in love with.

The next morning, I checked my phone and had a voicemail from Taylor. It was left at 5:30 a.m. She said how much she cared about me and that she didn't ever want me to hurt myself. What had I done? The guilt settled as I got my morning coffee down. I had hit the point of no return on this one, and knew that even though it was a lie, now that it had been spoken, it might as well have been a truth.

Megan came over later that day, and could sense something was wrong with me. I told her I was just tired, and she somehow believed me. I was so comfortable with Megan, but after that night with Taylor, I could not help but question every second I spent with her. Being comfortable with someone really means just that. It didn't make me love her, or even really like her; it just meant that I was comfortable, which wasn't enough to keep a relationship alive. The sex was amazing. She could always make me laugh. On paper, she was the perfect girl, but I knew that what Taylor said about the way I looked at Megan had a lot of truth behind it. I didn't love this girl. I really liked her, but she was never going to drive me crazy like real love should. I knew though, that if I didn't try to make this work, I might always regret it, so we kept on going.

Summer was over and I was about to head back to school. I knew this was only going to add even more strain on our relationship, but we decided we were going to beat the odds. We called each other every night and saw each other every weekend, but it still wasn't enough. We were fighting more and more every day. Little stuff, stuff that would never matter, became huge deals. It was awful. One day she just had enough. She finally broke up with me, which was upsetting, but also kind of a relief. I was never going to be the one to do it, and she knew that, so she eventually just did it for me.

It's funny how break ups work. Towards the end of our relationship I was so sick of her, but now that she was gone, I really missed her. I knew if I succumbed to my loneliness I would be leading her on, something I didn't want to do. So I drank myself to sleep and continued on with school, doing anything to keep my mind off Megan. This worked fairly well until it was time for winter break again. Winter breaks have never supplied anything good for me.

I spent more time with my family on this break than I had before. I spent a lot of nights just talking to my dad about life, and growing up. Learning from his experiences. I would go on hikes with my mom even though I hated hiking. I had a whole new appreciation for them as I was getting older. The first night I really went out was to a party at Taylor's house one night. She was having a little thanksgiving themed party, and everyone showed up.

The night took a weird twist when Taylor turned a corner and saw me talking to her friend, Emily. She blurted out "Oh!" and walked away in a huff. I immediately realized what she thought had just happened, and I chased after her. I grabbed her by the shoulder and whipped her around.

— "What are you doing?" I asked her.
— "Did you just fucking kiss Emily?" she asked me.
— "No." I say, laughing. She was not amused. "Even if I did, what do you care?" I asked her.
— "You're mine." She responded with no hesitation. The words she just let slip out sobered us both up quickly. I looked at her in shock.

— "What the fuck does that mean?" I asked.

— "You're mine?" She said again, this time as more of a guilty question.

— "Do you know how fucking selfish you sound?" I said to her.

— "I know. I'm sorry." She said. " I know how horrible that sounds, but it's the truth. You're my Thomas. "

— "If you want to make me yours, make me yours." I told her. "But if not, you have absolutely no right to care about what I do, or who I do it with."

— "I don't want to share you." She said.

— "Well that's not up to you." I tell her and walk away.

I left the house after that. I couldn't deal with her shit anymore. It scared me that I might just accept it too, and that's the worst part. She knew she had me wrapped around her finger to do with me as she pleased. I always thought that she might fall for me again, but I now realized that she never would because she didn't need to. I had become her safety net. I was her fall back plan, her last resort.

I knew if I didn't walk out of that house right then it would have only gotten worse. I had nowhere to go, no destination, but I lit a cigarette and headed in the opposite direction of Taylor.

Eventually, a mile or two later, John was randomly driving by, and pulled over when he saw me. I told him I had nowhere to go and he told me to hop in. We went to his apartment and smoked some weed for a while. I told him about my night with Taylor and he told me I did the right thing by walking away. I knew he was right, but just as I almost accepted what he told me as the truth, my phone began to go off in my pocket. Taylor was calling.

I hesitantly ignored her first call, but it was followed by a text message that I couldn't help but read. "Come back" it read. I gulped. I said I couldn't but she wouldn't let up. She told me that everyone was gone. That she didn't want to sleep alone. She begged and begged until I gave up. "On my way" I told her. I told John I needed a ride and he agreed to drive me back, but made sure to tell me what a mistake I was making. I knew it wasn't the right choice, but I told him there are some things you just have to do, and he didn't put up any further argument.

When I got to Taylor's, everyone had left. She was in her backyard smoking a cigarette in a beach chair by the pool. The house was a mess. I walked over and sat down next to her, lighting a cigarette of my own. I hadn't said a word yet. The silence was finally broken when she said, "I'm sorry."

I told her it was fine, and we continued from there. The conversation just flowed from there. I didn't have a strong sense of time, so as it began to get bright I was shocked. I realized that it had officially been an all-nighter. Taylor is the only person I've ever been able to do that with. We could just talk about anything, or nothing, and everything in between. There is no one that I could do that with quite the same as her.

We took it inside, trying to hide from the impending sun. I'm not sure exactly when we fell asleep, but I woke up next to Taylor on the couch a few hours later. We went and got coffee. It felt like a dream. Nothing happened, I didn't get laid, or prove anything to her. Just being around her put me at a calm I had not felt in years. I watched as she tried to get her much-too-hot latte down and remembered why I put myself through everything that I do. Her smile, her make-up from the night before, all of it. I wanted to see it every day.

I knew at that moment that I wasn't going to be able to give up until she was mine. I knew it wouldn't be easy, but I thought the more I asserted myself as an important part of her life, sexual or not, it would make the idea of losing me inconceivable to her. I knew that after the night we just had, she had to be thinking some variation of the same thing. At least I hoped she was.

For the next week or so I tried to play it cool. A text message here or there, but I was testing the waters to see if she would reach out first. I spent my days mentally planning my takeover of her brain and heart. I thought about mistakes I had made before, and ways to not make them again. It's funny how if you're "in love," all of these things that would otherwise make you a borderline schizophrenic seem totally justifiable. I finally saw a glimmer of hope that Friday night when she called to invite me to a party at one of her friends' apartments.

The party turned out to be much more mellow than I had expected. For some reason, I expected a lot more of a rager than five of her friends and one of their boyfriends in a small studio apartment in the valley. "Maybe this was a good thing," I thought. Maybe she wanted to really make me a part of her life.

I was thrilled, masking my boyish excitement with the excuse that "I just had a lot of energy that night." After a few hours she told me that she was going up to the roof to have a cigarette, as her friend didn't have a balcony, and asked if I would join her. I quickly obliged and followed her up the fire escape.

I sat there, a picnic chair across from her, looking at what was, in my opinion, the most beautiful face in the world hiding behind a cloud of smoke. We began to rehash every drunken conversation we had ever had. We eventually got to where we left off that night at her house, but this time, it took a quick turn, not in my direction.

— "I wake up every day and know we should be together" she tells me. I brace myself for the "but…" She continues to say, "I just know it will never work."
— "You're wrong!" I was screaming on the inside, but staying silent on the exterior.
— "On paper… you're perfect" she says. "You're the only guy I can be myself around. You're the only person I can just be myself around, and not worry about anything. We can do nothing and I'm happy."
— "How is that a bad thing?!" I blurt out. "Do you know how ridiculous you sound?"
— "I know, but there is more to it than that." She says. "The butterflies aren't there."

That single sentence brought my world crashing down. I finally heard the truth. It didn't matter what I did, or how I tried to prove myself, the butterflies just weren't there. There was nothing I could do about that.

— "You don't think it's because you know I will always be there?" I ask her.
— "Maybe" She responds.
— "And you don't think that if I walked away I would be the biggest regret of your life?" I ask. She looks down. Without raising her head she says,
— "I honestly hope you are."

That's it. All the cards are on the table. I thought about trying to kiss her, maybe one last flail at happiness but I don't even try. I flick my cigarette, blow out the last of the smoke and go downstairs.

I didn't say bye to anyone. I got into my car and drove off into the night. I didn't know what else to do. I drove and drove and drove until I was a couple hundred miles away. I could barely keep my crying eyes open at a certain point so I just pulled into a big parking lot of a local grocery store and fell asleep in my car.

I awoke at the crack of dawn, sweating profusely. I was drenched. It was a mix of the sunny, what I'm assuming was near San Diego weather, and the dream I just had. I dreamt a version of the previous night that went a lot differently than it unfortunately did. In this dream, *Taylor gave in, she accepted me. She told me how much she loved me, that she didn't know what she would do without me.* It was amazing.

After getting some coffee, I began my trek home. When I finally got back, I collapsed into bed. I dreamt again, of similar things. *A date. We got sushi. We talked, and laughed and kissed.* I can't be positive of this, due to my sleeping, but I'm pretty sure I was laying in bed, smiling like an idiot the whole time. I know I woke up smiling.

I made some dinner out of leftovers we had at the house and crashed again. Another dream. I didn't wake up all night. It wasn't until the next morning that I came to consciousness. I arose from another Taylor dream. I didn't know what was happening. I just knew that this dream world was a whole lot better than the one I was currently trapped in.

I was leaving to go back to school in a few days, but I spent the remainder of my break trying to sleep as much as possible. I was drinking any alcohol in the house. Shots of cough syrup. Anything with a drowsy effect was entering my system at an alarming rate in the hopes to go back to that dream. That world. *The world where I was happy.*

When I finally got back to school, I was focused on classes again, anything to keep my mind off Taylor. Aside from homework, and some social life, I was still trying to sleep as much as I could. The dreams hadn't stopped. Every night was a different adventure. I was carrying out a full relationship, in my sleep, but none of it was real. Taylor and I had not talked since that night, and I had a feeling that we wouldn't for a while.

After a few more nights of the dreams, I realized how weird what I was doing was. I didn't know how to put a stop to it, but I knew I had to do something. I decided to start channeling that energy into a screenplay. I didn't know anything about where it was going, or what was going to happen, I just knew the lead characters. I began chronicling everything that had happened between Taylor and I, and while I could have written an encyclopedia series with the amount of shit I had to say, I was doing it scene by scene. I fell in love with the process. Turning her into a character that didn't only exist in my dreams was the most therapeutic thing I could have imagined. One night I could be filled with rage, and the next I could understand where she was coming from. I understood everything better as I rehashed each experience.

Before I knew it, school was almost out, and I had a rough draft. I let a few people read it, wanting to hear some opinions. Everyone who read said they really liked it. That was all I needed to hear. I knew that this is what I wanted to do. I finished out my semester, and told my parents that I would be taking the next year off of school. At first they were totally against the idea, but after reading my rough draft, they agreed to give me one year to live and write, if nothing sold, I had to go right back to school. I agreed.

After telling some friends my plan, they all wanted in, too. Jeff, Max, Luke, and I, all interested in different arts, dropped out together, planning to, at the end of summer, move into a house and start our lives. School let out, we all said our goodbyes, one of us headed to Chicago, one to Korea, one to Colorado, and me back to LA. We could not wait until the end of August, when we would all get back and start our year of adventure.

Taylor and I were locked hand-in-hand. We were waiting in an enormous line for a roller coaster. I promised I would take her to an amusement park before summer was technically over, and today I made my half-hearted promise come true. I hated these types of things, but she absolutely loved them. It was hot and crowded, and all I could hear over the murmuring overweight couples of America, was her making fun of me for never having been on a rollercoaster. "If I want my life turned upside down, I usually just pick another fight with you" I told her.

I shot up out of bed, sweating, due to the lack of air conditioning. I kicked my sheets and covers off of me and flopped back down. "When are these going to stop" I think to myself. The dreams of Taylor and I had only gotten more vivid recently. In reality we still hadn't talked, but I heard her voice every time my head hit a pillow.

We'd been moved in the house for about two weeks now, and I had not written a word. We all moved into this place to work on our desired forms of expression, hoping to make it big, but all we had done is party.

I slipped into a pair of sweatpants, and tiptoed through our living room, cluttered with passed out friends, and into our backyard. I lit my morning cigarette and photosynthesized for a bit.

The house was beautiful; a twenty-year-old kid's paradise. We were living like rock stars, on our parent's dime, which was quickly dwindling. I had to get a job soon, because the cash I had been receiving from them was no longer existent. Part of the deal of me moving out like this was that I had to support myself. The only problem was that I didn't know what the hell else I wanted to do aside from write. I knew I wanted to be rich, but currently had no means of getting there.

As people started to wake up, they slowly gathered in the backyard to sit with me. We all chatted for a bit about the night we just had, and then most of the people began to clear out. The people left were the roomies, two of the girls who had spent the night with them, and Dave the Dealer, our weed guy. Dave said that he could drive one of the girls home, and also began saying his goodbyes. On his way out, Dave pulled me to the side and said "I know you know a lot of people out here man, if you ever want to take some product off my hands, I'll put you on deck." I was by no means a drug dealer, but I told him I would think about it. "I heard from some of the guys that you were struggling with paper, so I thought I'd throw it out there." This was actually very nice of him.

My roommates began to work on their separate projects, not suffering from the same creative block that I was going through. I showered and headed out onto the town to turn in some applications. Everywhere that I walked by, coffee shops, restaurants, smoothie bars, etc. were filled with employees that looked miserable. When I inquired about hours and things of that nature, I was told I could take weekend night shifts, and the worst hours I had ever heard. This was not what I wanted to do. I know I should have taken the jobs, any of them, and tried to make some honest money, but I wanted to write, and drink, and be a rock star so I called Dave instead.

Dave agreed to let me start selling some of his weed for him, and even though I didn't really know what I was getting into, he fronted me an ounce of marijuana. He gave me some perspective clients, and some leads as to where hot spots were in the city for people who wanted drugs. I wrote down a few notes, like I was in a class, and took off on my newfound career. The next day, while getting my morning coffee, I saw an ad in the coffee shop for a reggae band that was playing that afternoon, and thought "hmmm hippies sure love weed." I wrote down the address to the show, and went home to grab my product. By the time the concert was over I had sold the whole ounce. At $20 a gram, I had made almost $600. "Not a bad day" I thought to myself. I called Dave, and told him the great news. He told me that if I ever called him about "work" again he would leave me face down in a river. I took note and never made the same mistake again. The next morning we arranged to get breakfast and I remember how intimidatingly he asked me "You think you're ready for more?"

— "I think so," I told him.
— "You better be sure" he responded.
— "I am" I exclaimed. He told me to,
— "Keep my fucking voice down."

The next thing I knew, I felt something brush up against my leg and I looked down. A paper grocery bag had been kicked to my feet, and I looked back at Dave. "That's a quarter pound" he told me.

After we finished up the food we had ordered, first Dave left, and then I followed suit, grocery bag in hand. I walked by a table of two cops, my heart pounding through my shirt, but neither looked up from their bacon and pancakes. I got into my car and drove home, never having been so careful on the road. When I got back everyone was at the house, and Jeff asked where I had been. "Just out to breakfast" I told him.

— "What's in the bag?" he continued to inquire.
— "Just some stuff for the house" I responded quickly and bee-lined to my bedroom.

I opened the bag at my desk and removed the industrial sized zip lock bag. My whole room immediately smelled like weed the second the bag was open. I had been smoking here and there since I was twelve years old, but I had never dealt with it in this quantity. I broke it up into smaller bags, an eighth of an ounce into each of those little sandwich bags my mom had packed for the house. I put them all into a backpack I used to use for school and hit the town.

Over the next few days I had sold about half of the product. Mostly repeat sales to the crowd at the reggae show I had attended. The rest I was selling to guys and girls I met at parties. I figured the best way to get rid of this stuff was to go to where people wanted it. Supply meets demand at the point of interest. It was working pretty well. I had gotten rid of two ounces in three days and only had another two ounces to go. Dave had estimated it would take me two weeks, so I was determined to get it done in one. That's just always the kind of guy I've been.

In the corner of a party one night, I saw a group of guys smoking a blunt. The majority of the people at this party were white hipster kids in their early twenties, but these guys stood out a little bit. DeMarcus sat at the head of the group, tattooed from head to toe. He stood six foot eight, and weighed approximately three hundred pounds. This was not a fat three hundred; these were not McDonald's or Taco Bell pounds. These were jailhouse gym pounds. I ventured over towards their circle slowly.

— "You tryna smoke, Kid?" I hear from the circle.
— "On no, I'm fine, thank you though." I responded, regretting each word as they left my mouth.
— "The fuck you tip-toeing over here for then?" DeMarcus asks in a voice that could make a giant shit his pants.
— "Do you guys want any more?" I asked hesitantly.
— "Want any more of what?" he responded.
— "Weed." I said as my voice cracked. They all started laughing.
— "You slang, lil' homie?" Demarcus asks me.
— "I'm just starting." I tell him.

DeMarcus motions for me to come sit by him. I walk over and sit down. I am introduced to all of his crew, and they laugh at how white I am. We talked about dropping out of school, hustling for money, the ins and outs of drug dealing, and before I knew it, DeMarcus purchased the remaining two ounces from me at top dollar.

My friends were leaving in a second, and I was in a car with them, so I said bye to the guys, thanked them for their purchase and began to leave.

— "Thomas!" Demarcus says loudly as I walk away. I whip around. "You seem like a good kid, when you're ready to step your game up come find me."
— "Okay." I said even though I had literally no clue what he meant. I

chased after my friends who were already a little way down the street and got in the car.

Dave was impressed by the speed with which I sold his weed. He got most of my profits, but I kept a portion, and it was nice to finally have some money laying around that wasn't just enough for bills and rent. Dave started giving me full pounds at a time, and I was selling them quickly. Some would go to my reggae guys, but most of it went to people at parties, and Demarcus' crew. I felt like I was in a movie. I was always moving somewhere fast, adrenaline pumping all the time, making money, it was fantastic. It was nice too that I was just an average looking white kid, because nobody really messed with me. I was living the dream.

Nothing at home had really changed much, though. My roommates had a rough estimate as to what I was up to at this point, but I was never flashing the money or anything. I was stashing it all in an old shoebox in my closet. I sold most of the product at night, so during the day I was actually able to get a lot of writing done. My first screenplay was now done — a basic boy meets girl story based on Taylor and me. I spent the afternoon sending it to every agency and producer whose emails, or mailing addresses I could find online. It was untitled, and literally just chronicled Taylor and my true story from meeting to break up. The heart of the story came from the kid, based on myself, learning how to get over her and be happy, something I had not yet actually figured out. I sent out my last few emails and laid down for a nap.

Taylor was sitting next to me on the couch. We were both super tired. She was cuddled up in a blanket that I bought a year or so ago for my dorm room. It was one of those microfiber super soft blankets, and since we had started dating again, it had officially become her property. Her phone was sitting on the coffee table in front of us, next to my cigarettes, keys, and a pink lighter with a baby blue heart on it that she made me buy at the gas station. When Taylor's phone went off, alerting her of a text message, we both looked down at the phone, and I saw that her background was a photo of us on the rollercoaster at the amusement park. Her face was filled with joy and excitement, while I looked a little more like an about-to-be burn victim.

I realized in that moment, in that dream, that my dreams were starting to connect. It wasn't just the same people; I was beginning to follow a story line.

We went on with our day, getting some lunch at Taylor's favorite café in Santa Monica which was a bit of a drive to get to, but on a Sunday with the windows down, time seems to fly by. We went to dinner and a movie and then went back to the house. We opened an old bottle of wine I was given by a family friend at my high school graduation and got drunk in the back yard. It was literally a perfect day. We ended the night making love and passing out. Taylor was the only girl I could "make love" to. I could fuck, smash, destroy, or any other expletive kids were using, to any girl, but Taylor was the one I made love to, at least in my dreams.

I was lucid dreaming at this point, so I was making these decisions. I wasn't just watching as an invested third party. The only control I didn't have was the entrance. The dreams started wherever I was plopped into the story.

In the middle of the night Taylor went into my closet to get a sweatshirt because my body heat just wasn't enough now that it wasn't summer anymore. When she was trying to find her favorite one, she accidentally knocked over a *peculiarly placed shoebox. The box hit the floor and out came $17,000. "What the fuck is this, Thomas?!" she yelled. I jump out of bed and see the cash on the floor, and gulp, trying to find the words to begin this explanation. I sit her down on the bed, trying to make her understand but she is not happy. She doesn't break up with me, but she is not happy.*

— "Who do you think you are?" She asks me. "You're not the badass you might think you are. You're a nerdy goofball, and I love that about you."
— I have it under control." I say, trying to convince her, and partly myself too.

I had never seen all of it on the floor out like that. It was a lot of money. I promised her that I was only going to do it for a few more months until I had enough to last me for a while and then I would just focus on writing. She didn't agree or disagree with me. She passive aggressively took all the covers with her as she rolled over and went back to sleep. I laid there on my back, disappointed in myself that I upset her.

I woke up less sweaty than usual, but the disappointment had not stayed in just the dream. I was still very much in a bad mood. Of course, now that I wasn't asleep, Taylor was nowhere to be found. I hadn't even heard her voice for the better part of a year now. It was late afternoon and I knew I had to gear up for "work" soon. My phone went off and I answered. It was DeMarcus. He wanted some weed for a party he was having that night and told me to bring it to his house. I usually wouldn't do this, but he said he would buy everything I had, so I wrote down his address and got in my car.

I pulled up to the beautiful all white Hollywood hills mansion very confused. DeMarcus bought a lot of pot from me, and was always wearing jewelry and stuff, but even if he was just renting this place, it would be at least $30,000 a month. The place was massive. I knocked on the front door a little harder than usual I guess, because the door just pushed open, revealing a huge marble living room.

I announced my presence in the open living room in an attempt to not startle anyone that might accidentally shoot me. A topless woman, only wearing bikini bottoms popped her head around the corner from the next room. She was beautiful, a margarita in hand, she said, "Can I help you?" I told her I was looking for DeMarcus.

— "D!" she screamed out. "He's somewhere around here."
— "Tommy!" I turned around and saw DeMarcus, Cuban cigar hanging from his lips. "What's good, Kid?"
— "I got the stuff." I told him.
— "Great! Grab a drink, come to the back."

I nodded my approval of the situation and followed him into the kitchen. I poured a margarita and followed him into the massive backyard. A few of the guys from his crew that I had seen before, and an abundance of beautiful girls wearing close to nothing sat around the infinity pool. I found a seat next to DeMarcus and lit a cigarette. We exchanged some small talk about beautiful Southern California for a while before DeMarcus got down to business.

— "You know I could buy weed from just about anyone in this city right?" He asks me.
— "I guess" I responded. I had thought of this before, but figured he just liked me because I posed zero physical threat to him or any of his friends.
— "I chose you to see how competent you were at getting rid of your product. To see your work ethic." I couldn't tell if DeMarcus was about

to kill me or give me a trophy so I just sat there in silence. "I want you to start working for me." He told me. I had always wondered, but I had never asked what DeMarcus actually does. This house, the cars, the jewelry, it didn't just appear out of thin air, so I figured I would ask.
— "What exactly do you do?"
— "I supply Southern California with snow... year round." He said. I was confused as to what he meant until it clicked.
— "Oh!" I said. That would explain all of this, I thought. I tried to sell some weed to hippies and I ended up at Scarface's house. Fantastic.
— "How would you like to work for me?" He asked. I was hesitant to respond. "There's a lot more money in it than that little green you pushing." He says. I look around at everything he has, and I just nod.

Even though I felt like 8-Ball was probably rolling in his grave, I partied with DeMarcus' crew that night, getting wasted off the most expensive champagne I've ever tasted, doing coke for the first time in over a year, and ended up in bed with a girl that "D" told me he had already tee'd up for me. I felt like I was in a rap video for eight hours. It was awesome.

After our fun night of celebration it was right back to business and DeMarcus started me off just as Dave did. I started with barely any, and as I sold that I was starting to get more and more. This went on for a few weeks and I had already made more than I did in five months of selling weed. DeMarcus was impressed by my ability to get rid of his product and told me that if I kept up the good work, he had a big promotion in mind for me.

I continued to prove myself until the big day came. DeMarcus gave me my first "key to flip." "Key," as in kilogram, was where the big leagues started. The street price on a kilo of cocaine was upwards of $20,000.

DeMarcus gave me the product wrapped up into the shape of a brick. It took me a little time, but I used the client list I had acquired over the last few months, alongside some customers that D had given me and I was able to sell it all.

I was making a huge return now that I was selling it at this quantity, and I was quickly getting involved in a world of money way beyond anything I had ever seen. In a day I would be taken to lunch by a billionaire hedge fund manager, grab drinks with a talent agent, and meet secretly with what I was pretty sure was a hit man. Cocaine was a hot commodity, and I became the friendly face that was supplying it to this extremely varied group of clientele.

My phone was starting to ring with orders left and right, blocked numbers, numbers I had never seen, and I would answer them all, something that DeMarcus had warned me against. I was letting the money and power get to my head, something I should have known not to do from every rap album and mob movie I had ever seen. I was letting customers pick up from my house, because in my head, if they wanted it, they should have to come to me.

This mentality came back to bite me in the ass when I awoke from a Taylor dream to the sound of my front door being kicked in. I heard one of my roommates come out of his room and immediately get punched in the face. I grabbed a baseball bat that I had since I was kid that sat in my closet and slowly walked out of the room to see what the commotion was, afraid that it might be exactly what it sounded like.

Five men in masks stood in the living room, each with a handgun. They saw me and began to walk toward me. "Where is it?" I heard as I began to retreat toward my room. A shot was fired into the floor. Then another. "It's in here!" I screamed, trying to fight back the tears that were swelling up like a tsunami behind my eyes.

One of the men pushed me into my bedroom wall, the gun pressed up against my head, while the others rifled through the closet. I had three kilos and about $60,000 cash in there. They found all of it. I was struck across the face with the butt of the gun, and by the time I came back to consciousness, spitting up blood, they were gone.

I checked on all of my roommates. Everyone was okay, but very shaken up. It was my fault that this had happened, and while everyone was glad I was alive, they were not pleased with me in the slightest. The wanted to call the cops and I explained to them that they couldn't. You can't exactly report a robbery when the only things that were stolen were $100,000 worth of narcotics and $60,000 cash.

They were even more pissed after I explained that to them, but they were smart enough to understand that the consequence of doing the right thing sometimes made it the wrong choice.

I stayed up the rest of that night, knowing the colossal mountain of shit I was about to be in. I sat against the wall of my bedroom crying. I only dozed off for ten minutes or so, and it was not relaxing at all because as soon as I slipped into a dream, *Taylor was screaming at me, saying, "I told you that you were in over your head! How fucking stupid can you be?!"*

The next day, I made the trek to Demarcus' house to explain to him what had happened. DeMarcus listened in silence and then motioned for some of his boys to come over. DeMarcus had me explain to them what had happened, as well. They listened with sad faces. "I'm sorry" DeMarcus said, as his goons hoisted me up.

They threw me across the room and began to all beat the shit out of me. In between the barrage of punches and kicks my face and body were receiving, DeMarcus spoke loudly to me. "I can't have shit like this, Tommy."

The beating had come to an end, and I felt half-alive at best, finding it hard to breathe. The men parted like the Red Sea, as DeMarcus walked up to me. He pulled a chrome handgun from the back of his jeans and shoved the barrel into my mouth. "You have 48 hours to get that money back to me. One hundred grand, in a briefcase, by Friday at sunset, or I'm going to have to kill you." He removed the gun from my mouth and walked away without saying a word. The men followed suit and I picked myself up, limping out of the house to my car.

I didn't know where to go, whom to talk to, or even whom not to talk to, so I drove straight to my parent's house. I knocked on the front door, and when my Mom opened it and gasped in horror I immediately broke down in her arms. I cried for a good twenty minutes before I even began explaining what had happened. Right when I finally started to tell the story I heard the front door to the house close. My dad walked into the living room. He could tell that something was horribly wrong, but being the composed rock I had always known and respected, he just put his briefcase down and pulled up a chair. "Let's hear it." He said.

I told them in detail everything that had happened to me in the last few months, and how much trouble I had just recently landed myself in. They were shocked at my actions, but were very understanding and caring, considering I just explained to them that their only son was in debt to a coke dealer to the tune of one hundred thousand dollars. They even said they would figure out a way to take care of it for me. An emasculating, but life-saving donation, that would never be forgotten.

After we all talked for a little longer my dad asked my mom if she would excuse herself and give us some father/son time. She understood and left the room, kissing me on top of the head on her way out.

— "You need to get it together, Thomas." He said in a somber, disappointed tone. "You have so much potential, but it's like you are hell-bent on never realizing or reaching it."
— "I know, Dad." I tell him. "I'm sorry." He had heard me say I'm sorry a million times before, but I think he knew I really meant this one.
— "It's okay." He tells me. "You know you're going back to school now, right?" This was not a funny situation but I couldn't help but laugh at that.
— "Yeah I assumed so" I reply between a slight giggle and the tears that had yet to cease.

My dad arranged for his lawyer to drop off the cash at DeMarcus' house with a note apologizing and further disassociating me from their crew. I never heard from DeMarcus again, but I was still alive, so I assumed that he acknowledged my white flag.

I moved back in with my parents to finish out my time before heading back to school. I was starting to become a real homebody surprisingly. All I ever wanted to do was live, but I ended up biting off a lot more than I could chew. I found that not going out and drinking, or partying was not the end of the world. I cooked a lot of meals with my mom, and watched movies with my dad on weekends. I spent my days working on my latest script, a retelling of this past year of my life.

I was still spending each night with Taylor in dreamland. *She had forgiven me for my colossal mistakes, just as my parents had. She would come over for dinner all the time, befriending my mom, and getting my dad to fall in love with her. She knew he was hesitant to trust her given our past, but every time she took his dish to the kitchen from the table, or grabbed him a beer from the fridge, we could all see him softening. I was gearing up to go back to school, and Taylor was coming with me this time, something we were both excited about.*

I could finally drink legally, and I no longer had the desire to. I had gotten so much out of my system in the past few years, that I just wanted to be an adult already. I had already been twenty-one for far too long. My fake ID, purchased when I was sixteen, now said I was twenty-six. The most I drank was wine with dinner. This had been the mellowest summer of my life, and it was fantastic. I got so much closer to my parents, and began to enjoy the little things in life a lot more. I was not happy that I was about to have to go back to school.

School started in exactly eight days, so I had to start packing up all of my stuff again. My dad and I were sitting on my bedroom floor, taping up cardboard boxes and labeling them when my cell phone rang. It was a number I did not recognize so I answered hesitantly. The number belonged to a film producer, Jim Halway, who had been given my script by one of the many production companies I had sent it to. He went on and on about how much he liked it and told me he wanted to set up a meeting with me. I tried to contain my excitement and calmly set up a lunch meeting in Santa Monica for the next day. As soon as the call ended I started jumping up and down in my room like a child on Christmas morning.

My dad spent the rest of the day trying to not let my excitement get to my head, but had no success in the matter. He said he was proud of me and took my Mom and I out to dinner to celebrate, no matter what came out of the meeting. After dinner I tried to get to sleep as early as possible, but ended up just laying in bed thinking. When I finally went to sleep *Taylor was waiting for me at a restaurant table, glass of champagne in hand. "Congratulations, Baby!" She exclaimed. "I'm so proud of you."*

I told her that nothing was set in stone yet, but she told me to shut up. "Don't try to brush this off, cool guy. You're so talented, I'm sure this is your big break." She told me. I kissed her. I had the best, most supportive, non-existent girlfriend in the world.

The next day, I got to the restaurant before Jim did. I sat at a corner table of the restaurant in the closest thing to a suit I could assemble from my wardrobe. Jim showed up in jeans and a t-shirt, allowing me to feel extremely foolish. I always had this image in my head of "Hollywood Types" but Jim did not prove any of those stereotypes true. He talked fast and got right to the point.

"Look, Thomas, I want to make this movie." He told me. He went on and on about how I was "the voice of my generation." He apologized for whatever happened between me and the character that was clearly based off Taylor. He did not know how much of the story was true, or what really happened, but he said it was clear in my writing that I loved this girl. He had been looking for a story about kids, drugs, love and sex, and when he read my script, titled You; he knew this was the film.

Jim explained to me that he was an indie producer, so any dreams I had about big Hollywood money were non-existent for this project right now. He told me the most I'd make off the top for this project was $25,000. I had no idea what he was talking about, that sounded like huge money to me. I know I had made more recently in my little drug lord phase, but that was not sustainable. This was money that justified the worth of my thoughts, and nothing was cooler to me than that. I tried to play it cool and just nodded.

— "Do you want to make this happen?" He asked me. I quickly replied, — "Yes sir," like I was addressing a drill sergeant. He laughed and shook my hand.
— "I want to move quickly on this, I'll try to get my money guys together, and have some contracts and a check to you as soon as possible."

The next week or so kind of just flew by. I was waiting on phone calls from Jim from the second I woke up to the second I was with Taylor. I told my parents what was happening with the whole project, but it was not easy for them to wrap their heads around. I told them I was not going to be going back to school, and they were not happy about it. I told them that this was my first shot at starting my life, and that I did not want to waste it. They eventually understood.

The contracts got signed, and I got my advance check for the script for a total of $20,000. The producers and director kept apologizing for the low-balling on the price, but I was twenty-one years old, and that amount of honest money seemed like a jackpot to me. I moved out of my house again, getting an apartment in Downtown LA. The next few weeks were filled with contracts, getting everything ready, and the early stages of the casting process.

Before I knew it, I was in the casting sessions; picking people I'd never met to play people who were closest to me. It's a weird thing. I saw people who sounded like those people in my life, and others who looked like them. The strangest part of the whole thing was casting Taylor. No one matched up to who she was. There was something wrong with each of them.

I was being too picky, and the producers ended up casting a girl I never saw audition. Her name was Cameron Altman, and if I ever saw her audition tape, she would have been my first choice, too. She was a gorgeous brunette, with eyes almost identical to Taylor's. During our first table read I could not take my eyes off of her. If someone was going to have to be Taylor, I was glad it was her.

The movie was a slightly exaggerated version of Taylor and I's fall out. I wrote it to explore the idea of unrequited love because everyone I knew was tired of hearing me complain about it for so long. I'm sure by this point the keyboard on my computer was sick and tired of it as well. As we began shooting, my role in the process dwindled daily. I was doing punch up lines, and making small changes, but I basically spent my days watching my own story unravel in front of my eyes.

The part of the story I was the most fascinated by was Cameron's rendition of the love of my life. She was a talented actress, and therefore seemed more and more like Taylor everyday. The difference was this was a Taylor that I had control over. When I changed a line, that new line is what would come out of her mouth. Being the idiot that I am, I let this get to my head, and one day after we wrapped shooting I asked Cameron to come out and get drinks with me.

We actually got along great, and after a few drinks, we were stories into a conversation I had never imagined. She asked who the movie was about, and I told her everything. When I was done she told me of loves had, and loves lost. We continued this conversation until the bar closed. I would have invited her back to my apartment but we both had work the next day, and it was already unprofessional enough that I had taken her out. I behaved myself and just said bye without even an attempted kiss and went home to get some rest. *Taylor was not happy with me.*

— *"You can't take a girl out that is pretending to be me!" I knew she wouldn't be happy, but I played along anyway.*
— *"Why not?" I asked. "We actually had a pretty good time."*
— *"You know exactly why not, Thomas. You already have two of me, you can't have three." This actually made some sense, but I felt like arguing so I took the bait and hooked in.*
— *"I only have one of you, and that's you. The one that doesn't exist." She gave me a sarcastic smirk.*
— *"You know you are the real me's world, Thomas. Just because she doesn't fuck you doesn't mean she doesn't care about you."*
— *"If she cared then we would have probably talked in the last year and a half." This was the first fight imaginary Taylor and I have had. I finally understood the saying "everything that shines ain't gold."*

Taylor was fed up and walked out of the room. I chased after her, but when I couldn't find her I snapped out of the dream. It was five minutes before my alarm would have woken me up anyway, so I just got up. I showered and headed out to work.

Cameron and I exchanged flirtatious glances all day while filming, unfortunately catching the attention of Jim as well. Jim pulled me to the side at our lunch break and said "What the fuck are you doing?" I told him there was nothing to worry about, but I knew that was a lie, and so did he. He made it clear to me that my dick was not more important than this production, and that I needed to keep that in mind. I said I would, but I didn't.

That night Cameron and I went out for drinks again and this time we ended up back at my apartment. She heard my sob stories of Taylor and told me she could change all that. At first I thought she might have just been an actress looking to get in bed with a writer, and that did not bother me at all. It wasn't until she kissed me that I realized it was more. Her kisses felt just like Taylor's and that was more than enough for me to throw caution to the wind.

The next few weeks went off without a hitch. The amount of no-holds-barred sex that I was having with Cameron did not get in the way of finishing our shooting days, so Jim had nothing to complain about. The late-night booty calls turned into dinners, and then again into breakfasts. Before I knew it, Cameron and I were a couple, and I couldn't have been happier. Cameron had become my Taylor 2.0.

This was all great until one day when we got home from a little weekend trip to San Diego and I went downstairs to check the mail. After sifting through the thousands of pointless coupons, I had some bills and a sloppily written letter addressed to myself, from myself, as the sender. The letter to my future self had finally arrived. I didn't know what it was at first, but when I noticed the forwarding address from my parents' house, I knew it was the letter from that damn assignment. I didn't want to open it in front of Cameron, so I put down my stuff and ripped it open in the mailroom.

I got what I wanted, I guess. I used to think I wanted to see this letter again, but when I finally did, I couldn't deal with it. Nothing had changed since I was sixteen. Taylor still haunted me, literally. She lived in my dreams. I read through the four pages of bad handwriting with tears in my eyes. Just as I was about to be done with the letter, something fell out of the envelope. I looked down and saw the photo of myself holding Taylor, kissing her.

I went back upstairs and saw Cameron sitting on the couch. "Anything good?" she asked. I knew right then and there that it was not going to work between us, or anyone, for that matter.

— "Just bills and stuff" I told her. I walked over and sat down next to her. She grabbed my hand.
— "Are you okay? You look like you just saw a ghost."
— "I just don't feel well" I told her. "I think I might be getting sick." This was a blatant lie, but I knew she had an audition the next day, and I needed her out of the apartment to leave me with my thoughts.
— "Oh no! I'm sorry, Babe." She said with genuine concern. "Do you need me to get you anything?"
— "I'll be fine. I just need to get in bed." I told her. "Go home and get some good rest. You have that audition in the morning."

She kissed me on my forehead and left. I poured a gigantic glass of whiskey and pounded it down. Against my better judgment, I took out my phone and dialed Taylor's number. After a few rings, she picked up. "Hello?"

We talked for a few minutes, catching up, and I thought about bringing up the letter, but I decided against it. I asked if she would meet me for coffee the next day and she said she would. Hearing her voice was so good. I had heard it every night since the last time we had actually talked, but really hearing it live was like a weight being lifted off my shoulders.

I brought the letter with me to the coffee shop. I wasn't sure whether or not I was going to let her read it, but it really hadn't left my pocket since the second I opened the damn thing. Once we actually saw each other, it was like nothing had ever changed. We were sixteen again, laughing about stupid shit, chain smoking cigarettes, and not taking a second to look away from one another. After a while of hearing about her last two years, telling her about my movie, and going through each other's ups and downs, I showed her the letter and said, "I got this in the mail the other day."

I just handed it to her, letting her read it for herself. She had to do the same assignment that year, so she knew what it was when she saw it. I sat there, seconds feeling like minutes, as she scanned each page. I don't know what I was expecting by letting her read it, but it was just something that I felt like I needed to do. I had a girlfriend, one whom I really liked, so I knew nothing good was going to come of this, but I sat impatiently as she finished the letter and got to the picture at the end. She looked up from the pages, eyes watery, and lunged over the table to kiss me.

It felt like one of my dreams, but I knew it wasn't. I knew this was actually happening, and that it was wrong. I knew I should stop it, because of Cameron, but I just couldn't bring myself to do it. I continued to kiss her, and I didn't really stop for the next 10 hours or so. We spent the whole day together, going to all of the places we used to. We ended up back at my apartment, in my bed, just like I feared/hoped we might. After all of the shit I had been through with Taylor, this was our first time actually having sex. It was just fantastic. I had five years of built up anger, lust, love, and hatred toward this girl, and it finally culminated in that moment.

When we finished, I laid in the bed that I shared nightly with my "dream girl," feeling like a schizophrenic, next to my dream girl, having just cheated on possibly the girl of my dreams, and knew I was in for it. I knew nothing good was going to come of this, and that was only reinforced when Taylor gave me a kiss on the forehead and began getting her clothes on. "Where are you going?" I asked.

"Home." she replied. I tried to convince her to stay for a little while, but it was of no use. Taylor was never the sleepover kind of girl, but she promised she would call me the next day. I walked her down to her car and went back up to my sleepless night.

I couldn't face Dream Taylor after all of this, so I sat up all night, thinking of what I was going to say to Cameron. I may be a lot of things, but a liar is not one of them, so I knew I had to come clean.

I saw Cameron the next day, and told her everything. She was horribly understanding, and that only made me feel worse. She said she could hear it in my voice, every time I talked about her, and she knew this was coming. She told me I was never going to be happy until I got a real chance with her, and while she hated having to let me go, she was not going to hold me back from that. I would have much rather had her scream at me, call me an asshole and slap me, as opposed to recognize my faults so clearly and walk away from me without a tear shed.

I spent the rest of that day alone. I couldn't face anyone or anything. I couldn't tell if I was making a huge mistake, or doing the right thing. My mind was everywhere. As I sat on my couch, contemplating all of this, I accidently dozed off, having not slept in thirty hours. *Taylor was waiting for me, not happy at all. "What the fuck do you think you're doing!"*

— *"I don't know how you could be mad." I told her. After all, she was mad at me for being with herself.*
— *"You can't have it all, Thomas. Am I not enough for you?" She sat with her arms crossed, anger across her face.*
— *"You're the love of my life. You know that. But you are just a figment of my imagination. You are the sum of my memories of Taylor. You're my substitute for her."*
— *"Oh real nice, asshole." Taylor got up and walked away, vanishing into thin air.*

I woke up to the sound of my phone ringing, drenched in sweat. I looked at the screen and saw that it was Taylor calling. She came over and hung out again that night. We rented a movie and stayed in all night, eating our body weights in Chinese food, a similar night to one that I shared with Dream Taylor. My dreams' becoming a reality was no longer a metaphor, it was actually happening.

Taylor and I started to hang out more and more, and everything seemed to be coming together. After some rough cuts of "You" were seen, they received really positive feedback. The great response to my first film lead to me getting my first agent, a man named Michael Seething, who told me, along with all of his other clients, that we were the "next big thing." Aside from the total absence of Dream Taylor, someone I had come to know and love in a weird way, things couldn't have been better.

After a few more weeks of Taylor and I doing whatever we were doing, I decided to take the next step. I took her out to a beautiful dinner near the beach, and afterwards asked if she would be my girlfriend. It seemed like a childish thing to do, but it was my way of saying "don't fuck anyone else" while still being "romantic."

We talked about how much we have both grown and matured since the last time we really tried this, and after some of my finest convincing, she said "Yes." I missed Dream Taylor a lot, but if that was the sacrifice I had to make for this, it was well worth it. The only problem was that Dream Taylor had become my muse in a lot of ways for my writing, and while she was gone, I was not able to write a word. I would try. I would sit in front of my keyboard for hours pondering ideas, but writer's block is a very real thing, and even though I wanted to so bad, I couldn't get words down for the life of me.

It may have been that my writing came from a sense of control, or at least having control let me think I could decipher the actions and experiences of my past in a better way. It may have been that I felt crazy for having these dreams, and writing was a way of justifying what I was going through. Either way, with her absence, I had nothing. I had everything I had ever said I wanted, but I had nothing. I no longer had control over it. I was once again, floating about, just another one of the billions of victims of circumstance that populate this world everyday.

Even though I still had not written a word, things with Taylor were going great. I can't remember the last time we fought, and the similarities between the real Taylor and the one in my dreams were starting to poke their head out. The movie was out of postproduction, and had gotten into a few major film festivals, a feat my director was proud of beyond words. The first one was in a few weeks and the whole team was going, the director, lead actors, the producers, even Taylor, the inspiration for the whole project, and myself.

The first festival was in Utah. The film had gained a lot of hype due to our beloved director getting wasted our first night there and being detained on the red carpet, so our premiere showing had a line around the block. The whole thing was surreal. In editing bays, and first cut screenings I had seen my name on the screen, but really seeing it in a theatre, with all of those strangers, next to the love of my life... Nothing could compare.

For the first showing, I was seated between Cameron and Taylor, an awkward spot to be, but it was fine. Cameron actually told me she was happy for me, and in a week like this, where we were all celebrating, there were no hard feelings to be had.

The audience couldn't have been more in love with the film. Not just at that first screening, but at all of them. Utah, Australia, New York, and even France, we received applause for minutes after the credits rolled, each and every time. I was having so much fun. In Utah we were in the cold winter, and a few weeks later we were on the beaches of Melbourne. Taylor and I did everything together. I felt like we were a married couple, and unlike this situation with anyone else, that didn't scare me at all.

Dream Taylor had not shown up in a couple of months now, not since our last fight. I was okay with it though. Taylor had become my Dream Taylor, and that's really all I ever wanted. She kept telling me how proud she was of me on those trips, and even joked at one of my question panels for the film that "my next movie was going to have to be a romantic comedy at the rate we're going."

By the time the trips were over, our vacationing utopia began to vanish slowly but surely. Things were still going okay between us, but the city of angels has a strange way of distancing people. Nothing of any substance had changed, nothing I could pinpoint, but something just felt off, an intuition that, given our history, terrified me immensely. My agents were bugging me every day to write something new, or at least pitch something, after the buzz I had around me from the festivals, but I just ignored their calls. I didn't know how to tell them I was useless, a classic example of a writer that could not write.

This all went on for a while longer, until one day, I had a mental breakdown. I called my agents and told them to stop bugging me for a while. They were not happy, but said they would give me a little longer. I confronted Taylor about why she was being so weird, and she responded, just as she had in the past, with "nothing is wrong." A lie that fell on smarter ears than the last time she said it. I told her that was bullshit, and to tell me why she had been acting so weird. Our first fight since we were back together. She went on and on, trying to convince me I was acting weird and not her, but I wasn't buying it.

The next few weeks were submerged in whiskey and self-pity. I felt like an idiot for letting this happen again. I don't know why I had an inability to be satisfied or happy, but I just couldn't. I was drinking every day from morning until night. I started doing coke again, and the light that could be seen in my face just a week or two before, was long gone. The only plus side was that I actually wrote a little. Nothing good, but the fact that I was writing at all was enough for me.

Taylor and I were spending less and less time together. This was most likely due to the fact that I was no fun to be around when I got like that. When we would see each other, we were still fighting. I still sensed she was acting weird, but whenever I'd bring it up, we would just get into another fight.

One night, after a long day of doing nothing productive, and not talking to Taylor in a few days, I decided to actually go out and try to be social. My favorite bar in Los Angeles was a small place called Shivers. I have no clue what the real name of the place was, but it was nicknamed this early on due to how low they kept the air conditioning at all times. The place was never over sixty-five degrees and I always loved that. I took a cab there because I couldn't drive for the life of me, and I figured I would just have a drink or two. Five or six drinks later, I looked up from my empty glass and my eyes fell on Taylor talking to a tall, handsome, blonde guy I had never seen before. At first I thought maybe he was a gay best friend, someone consoling her for what an asshole I had been the last few weeks, but I quickly learned I was wrong.

I watched them from the other side of the bar, like a hunter stalking his prey, and then I saw something I really wish I had not. He kissed her. The kiss was one of those first few month kisses, the kind that's better than any drug, or sex, or money in the world.

With out thinking I approached them. "What the fuck? Who the fuck is this?" I asked at an inappropriately loud volume.

— "Thomas I'm so sorry, but they still aren't there." Taylor said to me, putting her hand on my shoulder trying to comfort me.
— "What are you talking about?" I asked. "What's still not there?" I was getting light headed, teetering on the edge of a complete black out.
— "The butterflies" she told me. "I thought they were, but they're not. I love you Tom, I really do, but I am not in love with you."
— "You don't mean that." I told her, hoping I was right. But I knew she was finally not lying, and that nothing had changed since we had this same fight at sixteen, nineteen, and again now, at twenty-two.
— "I do. I wish I could love you. I wish it more than anything, but I just don't." She knew how mean she sounded, but it just kept coming out. "What I love is how much you love me, that's why I keep coming back, but it's not fair. I can't keep doing this to you."
— "You think it'll be different with anyone else?" I ask.
— "It already is," she tells me, as she looks down in shame, grabbing the

hand of the man next to her.

— "This asshole?!" I yell. "Are you kidding me? What the fuck does this guy have that I don't."

— "Hey, Man. I think it's about time you got out of here. I can take care of her from here," he said to me, behind a self-entitled smirk.

The all too familiar feeling of my world imploding began to kick in, and mixed with the amount of alcohol I had drank, I completely blacked out in a fit of rage.

What I'm told happened was I punched the guy in the face. He hit the floor, but got right back up and knocked me down. We rolled on the floor exchanging punches while Taylor screamed and cried at us. People tried to break us up, but I was out for blood. When we were finally separated, I took a glass from the bar counter and smashed it into his head. The glass shattered upon impacted, and cut up both my hand and his head, knocking him unconscious. Again, I don't remember most of this, it's just how I'm told everything happened.

What I do know is that I woke up a few hours later, my hand bandaged up, in a jail cell. The cold hard reality of jail beds is not a comforting feeling. I had fucked up before, but never something like this. I didn't know at the time how I had even ended up there, but I knew it couldn't have been good. I took my phone call, and called my Dad. He was not pleased to accept that collect call, but he came and bailed me out anyway. While I waited for him to come get me the guard informed me on everything that had happened. I was shocked. I had never attacked someone like that in my life. I couldn't imagine how much Taylor hated me. I asked how the other guy was doing, and found out that he was still in the hospital, but that he should recover fine.

— "How much is my bail?" I asked the guard, already feeling guilty my dad was about to have to pay it.

— "It says here that with the possession of a controlled substance on top of your aggravated assault with a deadly weapon charge your bail is set at $50,000. You're lucky they're even letting you out before your court date.

I slunk down against the wall onto that hard metal bed. I didn't hear anything else the guard said. I began to cry. What had I gotten myself into? My Dad came and got me, but neither of us spoke the whole way home. I knew the mountain of shit I was about to have to deal with, but all I could do was go to sleep. I walked into my old bedroom in my parent's house and collapsed on my childhood bed.

I awoke to a knock on the door, and the murmur of voices outside of my room. I got up, still fully dressed, and opened the door. My dad, mom, and the lawyer that had dropped off the money at Demarcus' house stood outside of my room.

— "Welcome to my humble abode" I joked. Neither of my parents laughed, but I got a slight chuckle out of the lawyer, who I had only just then come to know as Richard Andrews.

— "You're not an average kid, are you, Thomas?" I didn't think this was the most professional first words from my lawyer, but given the last time my parents needed to call him, I simply responded,

— "I guess not."

— "I was able to get the security tapes from the bar, and you're actually in luck." Richard tells me.

— "How so?" I ask him, more curious than anything.

— "The guy you hit, Neil Gearhart, actually pushed you first, technically making what you did self defense."

— "Great." I respond. "I honestly don't remember a single thing that happened. I just remember waking up in the cell."

My mom starts crying, and my dad ushers her out of the room. He comes back; his look falls on me emotionless. A look much worse than anger or disappointment. Richard gets my attention again.

— "You do remember what happened, and he did push you first. Do you understand what I'm getting at here, Thomas?"
— "Yes sir." I respond. "I feared for my life, and I did anything I had to in an attempt to protect my well being."
— "Atta boy." Richard may have had no moral boundaries, but I could tell he was one hell of a lawyer.

We went over a few more things about my arraignment, things I could say and things I couldn't. Once Richard left, my dad stayed in my room for a bit, and talked to me for a while. He told me that he loved me, but that as I was getting older, I couldn't keep justifying these fuck-ups. He went on to say that he would never stop loving me, no matter what I did, but it would break his heart if I didn't get my act together soon. He said all my potential would go to waste if I continued to search for it at the bottom of bottles and tiny plastic bags.

That night, when I went to sleep, *Taylor made a re-appearance. She had even more to say to me than my Dad did. I listened to her yell at me, and tell me what an idiot I was until I finally shut her up with a kiss. I missed those kisses. There was something so comforting about those soft, sweet, imaginary kisses. I told her how much I missed her, she told me she did as well.*

— "Where the fuck have you been?" I asked her. "Are you just going to disappear from time to time?"

— "You can't have us both, Thomas." She responded. "You know that, don't play dumb."

— Well where were you these last few weeks since the break up?" I asked her. She stared at me for a few seconds before responding.

— "Even I don't want to see you like this." I look in the mirror and see the bar fighting, alcoholic, cokehead that has developed in the last few weeks, and I am appalled. I start crying a little and she pulls me in. I cry into her shoulder until I snap out of it.

When I awoke, I went straight to my old desk and grabbed my computer. My muse was back and it was time to get back to work. I wrote for hours, incomprehensible blabber for the most part, but it was good incomprehensible blabber. I did this for the next week or so until my court date, each night with Dream Taylor and each day in front of my computer, rehashing our conversations.

When it was finally time for my court date, Richard had prepped me enough, and when he showed the video in which I got pushed first, I got off on three years probation, because it was my first offense. Seeing the video, however, really upset me. I looked like a neanderthal. I should have never hit him like that, and I hate that I did.

Alongside the three years of probation, I had to pay some hefty fines and fees for damages, and Richard's time, etc. I had the money, but once everything was paid out, I needed a new job as soon as humanly possible. My prayers were answered when a day or two later my agent's called again, and instead of bugging me about giving them something new, they told me they had an offer for me.

A new show that just got picked up was staffing writers in New York, and they wanted me. Without any hesitation I told them to count me in. The job didn't start for two weeks, but I started packing that night. I needed to get out of this city, and my flight was both literally and metaphorically boarding the next day. I told my parents that when I came back I would be a new man and I left the next morning.

When I got to the big apple I got a hotel room to temporarily hold me over until I found an apartment. I unpacked some of my stuff, and got into bed, exhausted. I felt like I had only closed my eyes for a millisecond, not even a blink, but when I looked over, *Dream Taylor lay next to me in mis-matching pajamas, and gave me a kiss. "Did you think I wasn't coming?!"*

New York is one hell of a city. Ever since that summer I was here with my friends at sixteen years old I had said I would never live here, and what am I doing? I'm shopping for apartments. I visited a lot of the areas in the five boroughs, but I was pretty set on living in Manhattan. The writing team for the show is working out of Soho, so I'd already be right here.

At night I was going out and trying to meet new people, but it's not easy when you're starting fresh in a new city, especially in this world so polluted by social media and technology. How can you be expected to make new friends when it is such a time consuming process involuntarily keeping tabs on the people you already do know? Nothing is private or secure anymore. People need the opportunity to keep skeletons in their closets, those secrets are what we take with us, not the money, or even the moments, it's the secrets and the regrets. Human beings are selfish, self-aware, self-sabotaging creatures, and to think any different is just plain foolish in my eyes. Sure love exists, and it overrides everything in the end, but your first love is always yourself, whether or not you grow to like that person later on.

The bars in New York are a lot cooler than Los Angeles. The city never sleeps, and that makes a whole lot more time to get to know people, compared to California's ridiculous 2:00 a.m. last call that I had grown so accustomed to. I met some cool people here and there, got a few numbers, but I was really just looking for friends, trying to fall in love again was the last thing on my mind.

After about a week and a half in the hotel, I finally settled on an apartment building. I wanted so badly to live in a beautiful building in New York, with a doorman in the lobby, but I was moving into the fourth floor of a brick walk up, just off Broadway. Not the glamorous lifestyle I had always hoped for myself, but with what I was paying for rent, it might as well have been my own house in LA. It was a small space, but it was really all I needed. I bought a little couch, and a TV, and a bed, and I was set.

Work didn't start until the next week so I still had a little time to get more acquainted with the city. I called a guy I had met a few nights before, and he invited me to a party on some rooftop in Brooklyn. I told him I would meet him there, and I spent the rest of the day unpacking and organizing my new little cardboard box of an apartment. I tried to take the train there, but I still had no grasp on the city's "easy" public transportation, so I got off at a random stop and took a cab to the party.

It was awesome! The parties in New York are very interesting because they are either a lot wilder than those of Los Angeles, or a lot mellower. There was no middle ground. This one was on the mellow side. There were twenty or thirty people, but everyone was just hanging out, barbequing, and drinking some beers. Once I was introduced to everyone, I was greeted very warmly, which was nice. I talked to numerous people about their respective fields of work, and I was quite pleased to find out that apparently everyone in Brooklyn was an artist. This was comforting to the ears of a college dropout writer, who just blew the last of his money beating an aggravated assault charge.

Once people started clearing out a little bit, I stood at the corner of the roof smoking a cigarette alone, looking out over my new city. I was only interrupted from my peace when I heard "Do you have a lighter?"

I turned around to see a beautiful girl, with green streaks in her hair, holding an unlit cigarette between her lips. Even with the cigarette resting there, she was able to muster up a smile, resulting in one coming from me as well.

— "Of course." I tell her as I pull a lighter from my pocket and light her cigarette. "I'm Thomas."
— "Veronica." She responded, reaching her hand out to greet me. "New to New York?"
— "Just got here." I told her. "Still getting a feel for everything, it's a little different than LA."
— "If by different you mean better, it sure is." She says. "People here might be assholes, but at least they're not fake. I feel like LA is one big movie set."
— "I think that might be what I like about it." I joke. "Real sometimes just isn't as fun. That's why I write."

Veronica and I talked for the rest of the night, and well into the morning. We only decided to leave the roof and face the day when we had both run out of smokes. We had breakfast at some diner in Brooklyn, and then made our way back to Manhattan together. Veronica was a fascinating girl. She had just graduated NYU, with a degree in journalism. Talking to her was a lot different than talking to most of the girls back home. She was really smart, smarter than me, something that intimidated, and kind of turned me on.

We went back to my apartment, and after talking for a while longer, I went for it and kissed her. We kissed for a while and made our way to my newly-unfurnished bedroom. As things got a little more physical, she stopped and looked at me.

— "I'll fuck you right now," she said, "but I don't want to fuck you just the once. Does that make sense?" I had never had it put on my conscience like that. Usually I will try to have sex with a girl until I am told to slow down. I will try a little more sometimes, and then it's a yes or no, but it had always been up to her, whomever she may have been.
— "Let's wait" I said. I couldn't believe the words coming from my mouth. I had efficiently cock-blocked myself, but it felt like the right thing to do.

I wanted to see more of this girl, and I thought that given my previous experiences, if I had sex with her right away, I would get bored, and find a new challenge. She respected my decision, and could see how hard it was for me to stick to it. We kissed for a little longer and then she went home. I promised I would take her out that week. It took me a while to fall asleep after that, I couldn't stop thinking about the whole experience, and how intrigued I was by Veronica. It was about noon when I finally dozed off, and *Taylor was there, ready with some words for me.*

— *"Hey!" She said. "Looks like you sure had a fun night." I couldn't gauge how she actually felt about it.*

— *"I'm surprised you're here." I said. "You usually don't make an appearance after I've met someone."*
— *"I'm not worried about her." She said. "I only disappear when my presence is threatened."*
— *"And it's not?" I asked. "I actually think I might like this girl. I definitely do more than some other girls from the past."*
— *"I'm a figment of your imagination, Thomas. You're the one who decides these things." I hate when she's right, and she usually is. We talked for a little longer, and hung out until I woke up.*

I was still confused as to how she was still there, but it was nice to talk to her. I spent the next few days preparing for work, getting my brain back in writing mode. I was honestly a little nervous to start; I had never worked with other writers before. I had never had to argue ideas with anyone beside myself, real Taylor and Dream Taylor, and I lost most of those anyway.

The first day in the office was more of an introduction than anything. All of the writers met with producers and cast. The pilot was already written and shot, so we all watched and got an idea for what they wanted. I had read through the breakdowns on the plane, and while this wasn't my dream show to be working on, it was a job, and I desperately needed the money. Most of the other writers, a team of six of us, felt the same way. The people involved in the project are what gave me the excitement. The cast and crew were a great bunch.

We spent a few weeks story boarding and outlining the seasonal arc. We figured out the characters, and drama needed for specific weeks. It was a lot different than a movie; it was much more of an assembly line than it was an art form. The good news was that it was keeping me busy.

Between working there, and a few scattered dates with Veronica, my only down time was spent in bed, either with Veronica, or Dream Taylor.

Before I knew it, almost two months had passed, and while we were still polishing the last few episodes of the season, production was well under way and things were looking great. Veronica and I were hanging out often, and while we had not yet put any sort of title on our relationship, she was basically my girlfriend. We would hang out in central park for full days, go to dinners a few times a week, watch shitty movies, all the classic new relationship stuff. Even though she hated it, I would occasionally drag her to do some touristy stuff with me like visiting the empire state building, and in return I would have to go check out some small indie band in a dive bar with her. We had a good balance of sacrifices.

My big problem with Veronica and I, was ever since that first night, I knew Dream Taylor was right. I knew she wasn't "the one." As you get older, the reality of relationships and the future seem to come to the surface more often than they don't. I really liked Veronica, but if I wasn't going to end up with her, what was the point? What's the difference, in the long run, between what we are doing, and a one-night stand? These were feelings that I couldn't shake, and no matter what I did to try and block them out, I never took my relationship with Veronica to the next level.

When I first got to New York, the city enamored me. It was the end of summer when I got here, and there is not many things better than New York City in the fall. That being said, I was still a California boy at heart, so the winter was my worst nightmare. No amount of chestnuts roasting on an open fire, or the promise of a white winter was able to keep me warm. I was used to "cold" being around 50 degrees Fahrenheit. Veronica called me a wimp constantly, but I'd rather be mocked and called a baby than ever go through that winter again.

I somehow was able to endure the winter, and the closer I got to spring, each day brought promise. The show wrapped production, and while I could leave whenever I wanted, I stuck around a little bit to ride things out with Veronica. The show was not going to be coming back, and while I did love her, and she was an amazing friend, I knew I couldn't try to do some kind of long distance thing with her. I had to end it nicely, so I waited around until I felt the time was right.

The right time, or so I thought, was a dinner we went out to. We both loved Italian food, and I took her to her favorite restaurant thanks to my check from the show wrapping. We sat at a little corner table, and ordered everything that looked good. After we ate I ordered another bottle of wine, and decided to try to start the "me leaving" conversation.

— "Now that the show is over, I'm going to have to head back to LA at some point." I told her.
— "You don't have to." She responded like she knew this was coming. "I think you should stay here with me."
— "I love you, V. But I don't want to waste your time." She looked confused as to what I was saying. "If I stayed here in New York, I would be leading you toward a particular end goal that doesn't exist."
— "What do you mean?" She unfortunately sounded a lot more angry than upset. "You don't just want to see where this goes?"
— "I know where this goes, Babe. It's just going to get better and better, which is inevitably going to make the end harder and harder."
— "You can't think like that. Why don't we just live in the moment?" I could see a tear beginning to form in the corner of her eye. I brushed

her hair behind her ear, and used my thumb to put an end to the tear that was about to flow down onto her cheek.

— "I love you, but I have to do this. You are going to be better off. You are an amazing girl." It was not easy to do this, but even though she didn't believe it at the moment, every word I said was true. I put the cash down on the table for the meal, and I kissed her on the forehead, getting up from the table. I looked into her eyes for the last time, saying goodbye with a slow blink.

— "You know one day you are going to be caught without an escape plan, right?" She asked.

I took a gulp, and tried to respond, but could not find the words. I simply nodded, acknowledging her words as being completely true. She hit the nail on the head with that observation, she figured out my greatest fear, my fatal flaw. I had to leave after that, I went home and packed up my apartment. I was going to arrange for my furniture to be shipped to LA, so I just packed clothes and my computer. I got in a cab to the airport, hoping I could catch the last flight of the night back to dirty, stinky, sunny Los Angeles.

I was thankful it was a nighttime flight, because getting through security and to the boarding area wasn't as much of a nightmare as JFK sometimes can be. The boarding area for the flight, A9, wasn't packed at all. Most of the pending passengers were fully sprawled out on the seats, catching some sleep before the flight. I was so tired that if tried to sleep, I would have missed my flight, so I just stayed up, listening to some cliché break up music through my headphones. When a voice came over the intercom and announced that the flight was delayed forty-five minutes I looked around to gauge some of the other passenger's reactions, and my gaze landed on what I was sure must have been an angel.

A few rows of seats away from me sat a blonde girl, mid-twenties, in a cut up tank top that revealed a tattoo on her ribs. The tattoo was a Rod Stewart quote in cursive that read "that don't worry me none, in my eyes you're everything." I sat there, paralyzed, in complete awe of this woman. I took a deep breath, and then a few more, because I knew they were the last ones I would ever take without her being a part of my life.

I stood up and walked over to her, possessed by something greater than myself, because my brain was yelling "sit down, don't do this!" She had her headphones in, so when I walked up and tapped her on the shoulder, she pulled out one of her ear buds, a little puzzled.

— "Hi Maggie, I'm Thomas." She smiled at me and reached her hand out. I smiled back, touching her for the first time.
— "That's Maggie May to you." She joked. She let out a little giggle, and even just that was already too much... I knew I was fucked.

I sat at the table alone. The waiter should be coming back any minute with my third neat whiskey, feeling bad for me. The chair across from me at this table is empty, and Taylor should be in it. She was supposed to be at the restaurant thirty-five minutes ago, but she was still nowhere to be found. I said I would wait ten more minutes, but by this point I knew that wasn't going to change anything. She said she would get dinner with me so we could talk, but her absence is saying more than any argument could. She told me she was leaving, and after my finest convincing, she said she would meet me for one last dinner. I couldn't really blame her for standing me up though; she was, after all, a figment of my own imagination. It killed me that she might be gone, but it did mean that Maggie, which ended up being her real name, might be a little more important than I may have thought at first.

I woke up to the smell of coffee. I opened my eyes and looked over to see Maggie, in my boxers and a basketball jersey, sitting on the bed, holding up two mugs of coffee.

— "Thanks, Babe." I took the cup from her and took my first sip, sitting up against the headboard.

— "Were you having bad dreams again?" she asked. We had been inseparable since that flight from New York to LA, and she had become well acquainted with my ridiculous sleep world. I just nodded a "yes" and took another sip from my mug. I know this is jumping ahead a bit, let me go back.

When I got on the plane after meeting Maggie, I searched up and down the aisles until I found her. She was seated next to an old Jewish woman and she smiled as I walked up. After the old woman called me on my bluff of her being in the wrong seat, I came clean. I told her that I thought Maggie was one of the most beautiful girls I had ever seen, and that if I didn't talk to her on this flight, I might never get another chance. The woman stood up almost immediately, grabbing her purse from under the seat in front of her. She slapped my ass as she walked away and I sat down.

— "That's the kind of old woman I want to be." She joked. I couldn't wipe the big stupid smile off my face. Her face was like a pair of boobs to my inner twelve year old.

— "I can't wait to see." I said. She looked at me, astounded by my confidence, which came as a surprise to me, too.

— "So, Thomas, tell me about yourself." After I started, neither of us stopped. We talked for hours, completely effortless. By the time we were over Kansas we knew each other's life stories, and by the time we were over Utah we were kissing.

We talked about everything from childhood to present, and before I knew it I kissed her goodbye and promised, no swore, I would take her to dinner that week. It wasn't until I was in a cab on the way back to my apartment that I realized I didn't get her phone number. I freaked out. I told my cab driver what had happened and he suggested I call the airlines and try to sweet talk my way to her phone number. I rifled through my bag to find my plane ticket when I came across a folded up napkin with a poorly drawn heart on the front of it. I quickly unfolded it and saw a phone number. I let out a sigh of relief and held it up to show the cab driver.

When I got home I called her, and that lead to some dates, and then some more, and before I knew it, I was in the best relationship I had ever been in. I hadn't seen Dream Taylor since things started getting more serious with Maggie, but I was so happy that the worst it ever got was those empty dreams I had just awoken from. This was our first morning in our new apartment. Well really it was just my old apartment, but her moving in made it "ours." I knew just a few months was not that long of a period of time, but I was head over heels for this girl, and it felt like the right move.

Maggie was the manager of a boutique-clothing store in Hollywood, so every morning, she was out the door at eight to open up by nine. I, on the other hand, got to drink the coffee she made in bed, and then sit around all day in my underwear, doing miscellaneous tasks until I could think of something to write. My average day consisted of about three hundred paper basketball shots into my trashcan, two or three small lunches, a beer or two, and about four cups of coffee. This cycle would repeat everyday and was only broken when Maggie came home from work.

We would usually go eat somewhere or order some food in, and then, on most nights, went to a bar down the street from our apartment called Barcade. Both Maggie and I were teenage boys at heart, which made Barcade the perfect place for us. It was a happening Hollywood nightlife spot, decked out with a full bar and more arcade games than the richest nerd's basement could ever fit. From Pacman to Street Fighter, and from Hennessey to Pinot Grigio, this place had it all.

One night, as Maggie just got done beating me in some air hockey, a tap on my shoulder startled me. When I turned around I saw Matt, arm-in-arm with a beautiful girl. I gave him a huge hug.

— "How the hell are you?!" I exclaimed. I had not seen Matt since my freshman year of college.

— "I'm good, Brother. How are you? I only get the occasional update on you anymore." I'm sure Matt was referring most recently to my fight at Shivers, but I decided not to get into it.

— "Yeah." I laughed. "I'm doing well now though, just got back from working in New York for the last few months. Who's the lady?" I reached out to shake the girl's hand and introduce myself, but as she gave me hers I saw something that stopped me in my tracks. There was a big diamond ring on her finger. I looked back to Matt.

— "You dog... a married woman? Shame on you." He laughed a little and then pulled the girl in closer to him. "Thomas, meet my fiancé, Amanda."

After I was formally introduced, I introduced them to Maggie, and the four of us talked, drank, and laughed for the rest of the evening. Amanda and Matt had been dating for a few years now, and he popped the question six months ago. We heard about their history so far, how they met, etc. and even got an invitation to the wedding next month. I gave Matt some grief about not inviting me before, but since we hadn't seen each other in a few years I told him I understood, but that I would definitely be there.

Before Matt left, he did something I desperately wished he hadn't. He said goodbye to Maggie and I, and then after saying how excited he was that we were coming to the wedding, he looked at me and said "Taylor is going to be there, I hope that's okay." I gave him a half-hearted thumbs up and waved goodbye to Amanda. I held my breath until I heard the question I was dreading I would hear.

— "Who's Taylor?" asked Maggie. I looked at her and finished my drink before responding.
— "She's my ex." I told her. "She was my first love and all that nonsense back in high school."
— "Do you still have feelings for her or something?" Maggie went from intrigued to concerned very quickly.
— "Not at all." I assured her. "I have feelings for you."

She seemed to soften a bit, but she still looked self-conscious, or nervous, a side of her I had never seen. I thought about how crazy it is that Taylor could still tornado through my life like this, even though I had not seen her in almost two years.

The next few weeks it seemed like Maggie was trying to do everything she could to be a better girlfriend than Taylor was, and it was working wonders. I could have told her that all she would have to do is physically beat me, and she would be "better" than Taylor, but I didn't. I let her pamper me and tend to all my needs, and the truth is that it was keeping my mind off Taylor. In fact, I hadn't really thought about real Taylor since I met Maggie. Dream Taylor was the one I missed, but even she didn't compare to what was going on with Maggie right now. Maggie even came to dinner at my parent's house one night and met them.

They loved her, which was strange because they were always kind of protective over me after they saw how hard I fell for Taylor when I was sixteen. They always bugged me about bringing girls home, but I never would. I assured them that I was never lonely, but there was never anyone who deserved that next step. I finally felt like I was with someone who deserved to have me put that kind of trust in them.

Time was flying by while I was this happy, and before I knew it, it was already Matt and Amanda's wedding. It's funny how as you get older, years and time in general, start to move much faster, almost blending into each other. I remember as a child, periods of time seemed so clean cut. One year and then another, but this was no longer the case. As things stop being such a big deal, each event in your life seems to be a little less separate. They begin to turn into phases, or even stages in your life, not so much past, present, or future.

The wedding was in Malibu. Everyone we grew up with, along with family and friends, gathered at this beachfront estate. This was my first wedding of my childhood friend group. I always figured it would be me to go first, but no, to everyone's surprise, Matt was about to stand at the altar. Matt joked all through high school that "he would never get married" and that "it would be unfair to women world-wide if he didn't share his love."

While everyone was conversing, catching up, taking pictures and heavily abusing the open bar, out of the corner of my eye I saw Taylor, alone in the corner, babysitting a glass of wine. Maggie saw me look over at her.

"Is that Taylor?" Maggie asked. My silence gave her the yes that she was looking for. "Introduce me, I want to meet Taylor." Maggie started walking towards her and I followed suit. I had to catch up and get in front of Maggie so it did not look like an attack on Taylor.

As we approached, Taylor saw us and stiffened up. I gave her the friendliest wave that I could, knowing that no matter what; this was going to be awkward.

— "Hey!" I said as we got there. "How are you?" Taylor and I shared an awkward hug.
— "I'm okay, I guess." She said through an uncomfortable, forced laugh.
— "How are you? You look good."
— "Thanks. You do too." Before any of this could be mistaken for flirting, I pulled Maggie into the conversation. "This is Maggie. Maggie, Taylor. Taylor, Maggie." The two girls reached out and introduced themselves.
— "I've heard so much about you, it's really nice to finally meet you." Said Maggie. "He didn't mention you were so beautiful though."
— "Oh please, look at you!" Maggie smiled at the compliment, and I relaxed a little. It was weird seeing them next to each other like this. Just the sight of Maggie made me smile, but Jesus Christ, Taylor looked beautiful. I was watching my future and my past make small talk while I just stood in the background. Matt saw the whole thing happening from across the party and waved his hands to make sure I was okay. I gave him the thumbs up and he shrugged the situation off, going back to his wedding photos.

— "Will you go get us refills, babe?" Maggie pointed to her and Taylor's empty glasses. I gave her a slow blink, to see if she was kidding or not. She wasn't. I agreed and walked over to the bar.

— "I like your style, girl" Taylor joked. Maggie and Taylor both broke into laughter. I was not okay with what was happening, but if Maggie wanted to torture me and play this game, I was going to play too. When I got back with their glasses, I handed them their drinks and smiled. "I'm so glad you guys are getting along. I'm going to go find Matt. You two enjoy!" Maggie shot a look at me and I gave her a wink, walking away to where the photos were being taken. I found Matt just as they were finishing up the pictures with the groomsmen. Matt motioned with his hands to try and ask if I had a cigarette, and I nodded back a yes.

We snuck off around the side of the house and down onto the beach where we found a seat on some rocks. We lit our cigarettes and finished what was left in both of our glasses.

— "Amanda is making me quit." Matt was savoring every last bit of smoke in his lungs. I laughed, exhaling smoke up into the beach air.

— "You're lucky, I wish I had someone to make me quit." I ashed my cigarette into a seashell the water had thrown upon the rocks.

— "You're still young, count your blessings." I could tell the impending wedding was laying heavy upon Matt's brain.

— "You nervous?" I asked him knowing the answer before he even began to speak.

— "Yeah man, this is it. The rest of my life starts in an hour. That's a weird thing to think about. I love Amanda, but I still want to go out and be high schoolers with you again. I want to get in trouble and just write it off as youth." I could see it in his eyes. He really did miss the life I had been living since we graduated. The life that I now hated. The life that had done nothing but get me in trouble.

— "No, you don't. I've been doing it since we were sixteen and I promise you it is not as much fun as you remember it being. That's why I like Maggie. I can do nothing with her and it's easy. I'm happy. I meticulously compare every girl I meet to Taylor, and Maggie is the first one that seems to rank on a different scale. I don't need more of Taylor in Maggie, I actually wish Taylor would take on some of Maggie's better qualities." I was actually just realizing all this as I said it.

— "You don't still think you're going to wind up with Taylor? You don't think one day you're going to both drop all your shit and just live happily ever after?" Matt savored the last drags of his now cigarette butt and put it out on the rocks.

— "I honestly don't even know anymore, man. Of course I kind of still hope for that, and dream about it, but I don't know if it will ever happen. Sometimes I think how could it not? But other times I remember she said she would never get butterflies when she looks at me, and maybe I'm just a weirdo who has held onto his high school crush for eight years."

I hated hearing the truth come out of my mouth, and decided to stop there before I started getting into the fake relationship I was living out in my dreams. Matt was a great childhood friend of mine, but even he would probably have me committed to an insane asylum if I let it all out.

"You're not a weirdo, Man." Matt put his arm on my shoulder. "It was weird when we were young, but eight years later, that's fucking commitment. If you're willing to let anything make you sad for eight years straight, that's a sign of strength, not weakness." I thought about that for a second, and it actually made me feel a little better. I clanked my glass into his and pulled out another cigarette.

Just as I was about to light it, we were interrupted by a girls voice. We turned around to see one of Amanda's bridesmaids holding her dress up so she could walk faster coming towards us.

— "There you are. Let's go, you have to get ready, we're starting soon." Matt took a deep breath and got up. I stood up after him.
— "You got this." I followed them back to the wedding. I watched as Matt walked towards his future, each step closer to forever. I knew he was scared, but I was actually very jealous. I wanted that, I wanted to grow up, to step up and become a man.

I got back to the ceremony and sat down. When Maggie and Taylor found me, they were both super drunk. Apparently while Matt and I were gone, they decided to start taking shots, and they were now seven or eight in. We were all seated in the same aisle of chairs together, so they just plopped down right next to me. Seeing them next to each other put a lot of things in place for me.

Maggie, who was just as drunk as Taylor, was just ultra-friendly, and cuddled into me, giving me a kiss. Taylor seemed like the same drunk she had always been. Her eyes lost life, they just observed and judged from afar, completely separated from her as a person. I was really happy I was with Maggie, and while I was still afraid I would always be in love with Taylor, for the first time ever, in that moment, I was happier from just being near her and needing nothing else. I smiled at her and she smiled back, erasing all the bad stuff between us just like we always had done in the past. She motioned to me that she liked Maggie with a thumbs up.

The wedding was beautiful. Matt looked happy, as did Amanda. They looked at each other like they were in love. I looked over at Maggie during the ceremony and she was wide eyed like a child watching their first cartoon. I leaned over and kissed her on the head.

"That's going to be us one day." She didn't react visibly to it, but she grabbed my hand and held it tight, acknowledging that she felt the same way. Taylor heard me, too, but she didn't look over. She stared straight ahead, stiff as a board.

After the ceremony, the party started and everyone had a great time. We all drank, ate, and danced, and for the first time in a long time I felt genuinely happy. My mom called me and made me give Matt the phone to congratulate him. We really had grown up. This was the start of a whole new chapter in my life. I even danced with Taylor. We danced as friends, and as I held her waist I looked at her, and then at Maggie, and when I looked back at Taylor, I saw my best friend again. Not my nightmare, or my dream girl, but the girl I saw that day she toured my school. This is the moment I would usually run for the hills. Run from Maggie, run from Taylor, but I didn't. I finished the dance, and went back and kissed Maggie. We left, went home to our apartment, and got in bed.

Maggie and I were happy, mainly because we didn't have to try to be happy, it was effortless. She was working at the store, and I was writing again. I was finally writing something I cared about, and not just forcing words out. I started writing a new movie about a guy who goes back in time to try and figure out where things fell apart with the love of his life, just to figure out they just weren't meant to be in the first place. I have really only been able to write what I know.

My delete button has started to stick to the keyboard. It had seen a lot of abuse recently. I was almost done with the script, but as usual, I was having trouble with the ending. I've never been able to wrap things up well. A problem not only in my writing, but also in my real life. That's why Taylor is still a factor in my life, and Dream Taylor, and my whole past, in general.

This has been prevalent even more so recently, because since the wedding, Taylor has actually been in my life a lot more than I would like her to be… which is not at all. Taylor and Maggie really did like each other, and they had even gone out for drinks a few times since.

Maggie was still at work, so I was just sitting around in my boxers trying to write. My agents were bugging me non-stop for the first draft, but I couldn't get myself to end the story in a way that I liked. I gave up for the day, closed my computer, took off my socks, the only article of clothing I had on aside from underpants, and laid down on the couch for a nap.

When I awoke, Taylor and Maggie were standing over me, laughing. I was so confused. I reached out and poked Taylor in the stomach to see which version of her she was.

"What the fuck are you doing?" She asked. I now knew this wasn't a dream, it was reality... or depending on your understanding of my past, a nightmare. Taylor and her had gone out to eat after Maggie got off work, and now Taylor was just leaving, much to my relief. She said goodbye to both of us and left.

— "I need to talk to you about something." Said Maggie. Not my favorite words to hear from a girl's mouth, ever.
— "What's up?" I asked. She took me by the hands and sat us both down on the couch. I prepared for the worst.
— "Where do you see this going?" This conversation was not going to end well, I could just feel it.
— "Is this about something Taylor said to you? You can't let her get in your head. I know you guys are friends now, but she will try to destroy me, I promise you."
— "It's not about Taylor." She seemed uneasy. She could barely look me in the eye.
— "Then what is it?!" It suddenly dawned on me. "Are you breaking up with me?" I asked.
— "I'm pregnant." She said after a moment of silence. I sat back, I didn't know what to say. I just clenched her hands tighter, and began to tear up.

Since I was very young I had always said how much I couldn't wait to be a dad, but now that the bomb had officially been dropped, I didn't know how to feel. I immediately felt like I was in a bubble. Everything sounded different, felt different; I didn't know what to do.

I was on the verge of asking "how did this happen?" But I refrained from doing so. Before the words could come out of my mouth, I quickly remembered the night of the wedding.

Maggie and I had both drank a lot, and by the time we got home, for lack of a better phrase, it was on. We were always pretty good about wearing condoms, since she didn't like taking birth control pills, and even this drunk, I remembered to put one on. It wasn't until after the sex, when I noticed the whole condom was at the base of my penis. I didn't know at what point it had ripped, but we both joked about it happening because the sex was so good, and brushed it off.

It no longer seemed very funny. Maggie looked terrified. I wanted to keep the conversation moving, making her feel comfortable, so I began it the only way I knew how, from watching movies and television shows.

— "What do you want to do?" I asked. I knew there was only really two, or three options in a situation like this, but I was still surprised when she responded.
— "I think we should abort it." The words landed upon my ears heavy and cold. I thought she may have been joking at first.
— "Completely?" I asked, like an idiot. She no longer looked frightened, but angry.
— "No, Thomas. We'll only abort this one half-way." She was glaring at me, but I couldn't stop smiling that she still had the quick sarcasm I loved so much about her.
— "Are you dead set on that?" I asked. "You don't want to explore any other options?"
— "We can talk more about it tomorrow. I'm just really scared right now." She was beginning to tear up. I laid down on the couch and held

her close. I held her until she fell asleep. I couldn't fall asleep for the life of me though. All I could think of was that this was the first night we ever spent as a family.

I don't know when I finally fell asleep, but I woke up alone. It was noon. I got up and tried to call Maggie, but her phone was off. I showered and made myself a cup of coffee. Finally after three more calls and another voicemail, I got a little nervous, so I tried to get some writing done. Naturally, I barely typed more than a sentence.

After about thirty minutes of staring at my computer, I heard the front door creak open. Maggie stood in the doorway, crying.

— "What's going on, Babe? Are you okay?" I slammed my computer shut and rushed over to her. She sniffled back some tears and took a deep breath. She looked me in the eyes and said, "I did it."
— "Did what?" I asked. I was so confused. I really had no idea what she did until she said it.
— "It's gone." She was staring at me to gauge my reaction, which I still hadn't had yet. I understood what she said, but it didn't really hit me until I involuntarily threw my fist out, smashing it into the wall.
— "Are you fucking kidding me, Maggie?" I asked as I pulled my hand from the wall. She looked scared. "How could you do this?"
— "I told you it's what I wanted to do!" She began hysterically crying out of fear and sadness.
— "We said we would talk about it." I couldn't even look at her. I just walked out of the apartment. I knew she needed me, but I couldn't be who she needed me to be in the state that I was in.

I went to a bar, and had a few too many drinks. I needed to talk to someone, but I realized I didn't really have many friends when Matt didn't answer. I had a lot of people I was friendly with, but the only person who was really there for me was Maggie, who I just left sad and alone. Instead of going home right then and there, I continued to drink.

I had been there for about seven hours when the barkeep told me I needed to go home. Even after I told him I wasn't welcome there tonight, he told me I had to go. I said fine. I walked outside of the bar and waved a cab down, an unusual feat in the city of Los Angeles. He took me to the apartment, and as we got there, I realized I was out of cash.

I tried explaining to the driver in slurred, broken English, that he now knew where I lived, and he could come pick up the money tomorrow. He wanted nothing to do with that plan. It was only twelve dollars, but he began to take his phone out and said he was calling the police. I freaked out, taking his phone out of his hand and smashing it on the ground outside of my window. We both jumped out of the car, screaming at each other. He was about to hit me, and he had the right to.

"Stop!" We both heard the yell and turned to see Maggie, hair-up, in pajamas, running out of the apartment. She paid the guy $20 for the ride, and gave him an extra $200 for his phone. He thanked her and left, telling her she should leave me, as I screamed obscenities at him from the curb Maggie sat me down on.

"Get your ass inside right now." Maggie was no longer sad, or vulnerable, she was furious with me, and just the thought of the scolding I was about to receive made me sober up a little. I walked, tail between my legs, into the apartment.

We sat in the living room and tried to talk, but I couldn't even look at her the same. I was heartbroken. I had always been pro-choice, and all that, but I felt like I was speaking to a murderer. All I could hear was my imaginary son's laugh. When she started to cry again, I snapped out of my drunken, selfish, gloom and comforted her. I had seemingly forgotten that while this was hard on me, what she must be going through had to have been so much worse.

After that we were able to actually have an adult conversation, and we both said what we needed to. She told me how she wasn't ready to bring a person into this world, and when she does, she plans on making it her life. It wouldn't be fair to the kid, or to her, to try and do that now. I told her I understood and I just felt betrayed that she went behind my back. She apologized and we made up. That was the thing I liked about Maggie and I, no matter what, we were always able to make up.

Before we finally fell asleep we told each other that we loved each other, but I prefaced mine, saying I need some time to bounce back to normal, and that while I did love her, she really hurt me, and it was going to take more than a day. She understood.

— *"Are you okay?" I rub my eyes and open them to see Dream Taylor sitting across from me at a coffee shop.*
— *"Haven't seen you in a while." I hadn't seen Taylor in months, and she didn't look any different.*
— *"Something told me that you needed someone to talk to." She held my hand, looking into my eyes like she actually cared. It was really nice.*
— *"That's strange." I joked.*

I knew why my subconscious had brought her back up now, and why she had been absent for so long. Dream Taylor comes around when I need someone, when I can't handle things myself. People attract who they think they deserve. When I feel hopeless I bring back that ghost of the person who makes me feel the most hopeless. That's why a girl who grew up with an abusive father will find the abusive drug-addict in a crowd of a thousand guys. We allow our futures to happen and blame it on other things.

Luckily for me, even though it was a wildly unhealthy way to deal with my issues, Dream Taylor was nothing like the real Taylor, and she was actually able to help me. She told me it wasn't the right time right now, but when it was, I was going to be an amazing father. She said that if I cared for a child even half as much as I did her, that kid would luckiest kid in the world. The whole coffee shop started to smell like bacon, and then all of a sudden I was awake.

Maggie had started making me my favorite breakfast. I sat and ate with her, and then went out to go write. I needed a change of scenery. Due to the dream I had just woken from, I decided on a coffee shop.

As I sat there, coffee in hand, trying to figure out the ending to this damn story, I heard, "Hey, you!" I whipped around to see Taylor, paying for her coffee. I pinched my leg as hard as I could to see if I was dreaming still, and I wasn't.

"Hey!" Taylor looked better than she had in years. Not hotter, or sexier, but healthy. "What're you doing here?" Taylor held up her coffee to answer my question, giving me a sarcastic smirk. "I'm just killing some time before a lunch meeting. Mind if I join you?"

I kicked the chair out from the other side of the table I was sitting at. She came and sat down. "What's new?" She asked. I began to try and explain everything that had happened in the last few days, but Taylor stopped me.

"Whoa. This seems like a much longer conversation than the thirty minutes I have before this meeting. Why don't we meet for a drink tonight and actually catch up. I miss my best friend." She smiled and I melted. Even though it was a horrible idea, I agreed to meet her that night at a local bar.

Maggie went to work when I went to the coffee shop, so I finished a few more hours of writing, mostly correcting older stuff, and then went home and showered before meeting Taylor. I left Maggie a note that just said I would be back later, and I headed out.

I sat at the bar and ordered two whiskeys, waiting for Taylor. When she finally got there she looked stunning. I waved like an idiot to get her attention even though the bar was not packed at all. She came and sat down, downing her glass and ordering another one before she was even situated. I followed suit.

We drank and talked, and I told her everything that had happened. She was incredibly supportive and sweet. She told me most of the things that Dream Taylor had. She was actually being the person I had always wanted her to be. The plethora of drinks we had, plus how well our catching up was going felt just like old times.

It felt so good that before I knew it, we were in the back corner of the bar making out. This led to us leaving together, and going back to her place.

That led to me sleeping there, and that led to me waking up the next morning with a horrible hangover, and feeling guiltier than I ever had.

I got up and washed my face. Taylor was still fast asleep in bed. I thought about waking her up, but I knew where that would head, so I just left. I got coffee on the way and tried to compose myself before heading back into my home with Maggie. I had my first cigarette in weeks, and took the brave steps into my front door, praying that Maggie was asleep.

She wasn't. I walked in and Maggie was sitting at the kitchen table. She didn't look happy whatsoever. I assumed it was because I was out all night.

— "What's up?" I asked her. She still had not said a word to me since I arrived, which seemed a little strange.
— "You tell me, Asshole." Maggie threw her phone to me, catching me off guard. I barely caught it. I looked at her, and then to the phone where I saw a picture of Taylor and I kissing. It was taken at the bar the night before, by one of her friends who I must have not noticed before I made any life-altering mistakes. I put the phone down on the counter, taking a breath.
— "Listen to me." I tried to begin an apology/excuse, but Maggie cut me off right from the get-go.
— "Get out!" she said sternly. "If you ever want to see me again, you need to leave right now."

It was my apartment. I think she may have forgotten that, but regardless, I was in the wrong, so I left without saying anything. I was exhausted, and all I wanted to do was sleep, so I found a motel nearby, paid $35 and crashed.

I woke up eight hours later, just late enough to be the evening, so I decided to try my luck at going home again. I knocked on the door first, as a warning, and then I unlocked it. I called out Maggie's name, but I got no response. I searched the house, and most of Maggie's stuff was gone. I gulped. I knew this was a bad sign. I walked into the bedroom, where I saw a note laying on the bed.

I love you, Thomas, I really do. I want to be with you, but you won't let that happen right now. You need to work your shit out before you can be with me, or anyone. I wish I could help you, or tell you what that shit is, but I don't know. I don't know why you are so determined to be unhappy. You do this stuff just to be a bad guy, to convince yourself you're a bad guy, but you aren't. You are a sweet man. You are loving and caring, and one day, you will make a girl very, very happy. I don't know if that girl will be me or not, but I need you to be able to let love into your life, not just chase after the idea of it.

Sincerely,
Maggie

I cried as I finished the letter. I put it down and grabbed my phone to call her, but my attempts were answered by a voicemail message. I knew that everything she said was true, and that was the worst part.
I called Maggie every night for a while, but she never answered. I

couldn't blame her, I knew, just like she knew, that I still wasn't ready. I was getting better though. At first I was drinking myself to sleep every night, trying to call her, and then Taylor when she didn't pick up. Neither would answer. I felt pathetic, but I had finally gotten to a place where I wasn't drinking at all and I was leaving my phone alone. The only other person aside from occasional calls to my parents that I was talking to was Dream Taylor, but even she wasn't coming around much. I didn't need her, the only person I needed to confront or figure things out with was myself.

I finally finished the script, and sent it off to my agent, and manager. Most of the feedback was pretty good, but even though I finally found an ending, everyone thought it needed more edge. A different, darker, ending... or maybe a good old-fashioned plot twist. I laughed, thinking, "That is what used to be wrong with me." My story was a love story, and love stories should not have complicated endings. The middle can get rocky, sure, but the endings should be smooth. I always made plot twists and edgier decisions in my real life, and it had led me nowhere. I ended up changing the ending for business sake, but I finally got some real insight, and that was a lot more important to me than if this script sold or not.

Twenty-six was not a very eventful year for me. I spent my birthday alone, which upset my parents greatly. When I told my dad that I didn't do anything to celebrate he called me a pussy and took me out that night. We got dinner and drinks at a local restaurant, and talked for hours. We started with the basics, but as the drinks flowed through us, our conversation got deeper and deeper. I told him about everything that had happened with Maggie and Taylor (whom he was sick and tired of hearing about.) After he heard about everything, our conversation turned into much more of a lecture.

— "You're getting too old for this shit." He told me. "It's time to be a man, son. I've told you a million times that you have so much talent, and so much potential. I'm not the only one who sees that, but you're never going to allow someone to appreciate it until you appreciate it yourself."
— "Yeah, and who is that going to be?" I asked him like a smart ass, even though I was only further proving his point.
— "You really want to play this game?" He asked me. "That Maggie girl is perfect for you."

— "Yeah well she doesn't want anything to do with me right now." I tell him as I slouch back in the booth.

— "Oh, boo-hoo, Thomas. Cry me a fucking river. If you wanted to get her back, you would. I've never seen you take no for an answer when it's not one you are willing to accept."

His words landed like an anvil atop my Wiley Coyote. "What's wrong with me?" I asked.

"You're measuring system of self-worth is based on how that whore, excuse my language, feels about you. You purposely fuck up so that she can be right. In the back of your head you think that if you can justify her actions, you'll be able to manipulate them one day. Well, news flash, Thomas, you can't!" He took a sip of his drink, relieved that he said something he has wanted to say for years.

I actually took in what was said in that conversation, and we were able to finish our meal up nicely. I told him I loved him, and that I really listened to him this time. I don't know if he believed me or not, but I meant what I said. I knew I needed to say goodbye to the old me, or at least to my old way of thinking.

After that dinner my agents found a private investor to give me an advance on my next screenplay. It was enough to get me through a few months, which was perfect because the lease on my apartment was done anyway. I had always wanted to live an old Hollywood writer cliché, so I locked myself up in the Chateau Marmont and got to work on my next project. It was a character piece, naturally, and I decided to make it darker than anything else I had ever written.

I changed things around, but it was once again, similar to the story of my own life, but this time it spanned longer than just Taylor. It spanned a man's early life. It ended with a suicide, which seemed appropriate due to my recent choice to kill my old way of thinking. It was a dark metaphor, but one close to my heart.

I went through my normal process of writing and re-writing, and loving and hating my work. The difference this time though was that I wasn't doing anything else. I wasn't really talking to anyone else. The people I spoke with the most were my parents, the room service operator, and Taylor in my dreams. That is the only reason I was able to finish the whole script in two and a half weeks. I was fighting against both the clock and my wallet.

I would go down and try to talk to people at the bar, but I just didn't care any more. I didn't want anything short of what I had with Maggie. Quite frankly, I didn't want anyone else besides her. It's a funny thing, when you meet the right girl; she becomes your best friend. It's a great thing, but it's also very rare, and very hard to preserve. It's so easy to let childish shit get in the way of your future, it doesn't matter how old you are.

Dream Taylor had been more prevalent than ever during this process, but it was a whole new person, or at least a whole new perception of her. I made it clear to her that I didn't need her there anymore. She argued that I was still the one bringing her up, which when I thought about it, was true. I think I was still bringing her around because I needed closure, I needed to end my relationship with her, but it was going to be easier this way than with the real Taylor. I had control over this Taylor in a sense, and once I had said what I needed to, she actually started changing a bit.

Even once the script was done, and I was back in a normal apartment, Dream Taylor was there every night. We had developed a whole new dynamic in our make believe relationship. She really listened to what I needed to say, and she even had great advice for me. We were no longer a couple, or in between a back and forth relationship. We were finally actually friends. There were a few times where I kissed her, and there were times where I took it a little farther than that, but I finally had someone I didn't need, but rather someone that I just had. Through this new relationship I was able to learn a lot about myself. I felt like I was actually maturing for the first time in years.

The script, even though it was written very quickly, was extremely well received. My agency loved it. The investor that gave me the advance loved it, and said that he was ready to fully fund the project. I didn't know exactly where they were in that process, but my agent assured me that big things were to come. I didn't know what they had in mind, but I did mention the story was very dear to my heart, and if given the option, I would love to direct it.

I started working out for the first time in my life. I just started trying to do things for me. I had spent my whole life thus far, so caught up in other people; I knew that during this weird stage, the first person I needed to rekindle my relationship with was myself. I was always so self-destructive, and now that I was over the hump, or so I hoped, I figured I could maybe start balancing some of the partying and heartbreak out with some hikes and clean eating.

Twenty-six may have not been a very eventful year in my life, but it was easily one of the most important. I really became who I am today during that year, and I had my dad, Taylor, Dream Taylor and Maggie to thank for that.

No decisions had been made about casting, or production or anything, but the investors had put money into an LLC for the film. This started out the initial process to start trying to make this film, and it meant that I got paid for the script itself. I used the money to pay off any debt I had left, take care of the year's lease on my apartment, and most importantly, cut a big check to my parents.

Raising a child is a very expensive task, and raising me, with the trouble I got in to, was even more expensive. I would never be able to pay my parents back for everything they ever did for me, but I could at least try to start, so that's what I did. They were very appreciative, and while I know part of them wanted to not take it, it was more of a lesson for me than it was a present for them.

My present to me was an English bulldog puppy that I bought and named Henry. I had always loved dogs, and now that I was a little more mature and responsible, I decided I could finally take care of one. Henry was great. I was still as lonely as ever, Maggie and I still weren't talking, but Henry made everything a little easier for me. He never offered much in terms of advice, but when I needed him to sleep on the bed or be cute, he was happy to oblige.

I knew that the next step I was going to have to take was to talk to Maggie. I didn't know if she was going to take me back, or if that's even what I wanted, but I needed to speak with her again. I tried calling her a few times, but when those attempts were not returned, I put it on the back burner again. I knew when it was right it would work out, and clearly, this was not the time yet. There was more I had to take care of, and while I wasn't sure what those things were yet, I knew they were there.

After some more months of my haunting dreams, I decided to call Taylor again. This was probably a bad idea, but I had no one anymore, and honestly, I had always been a glutton for terrible choices. I had no intention of trying to pursue Taylor sexually anymore. I just wanted to have someone around me. That's the funny part about Taylor; even after all the shit we had put each other through, I never hated her. I don't think I ever could.

We finally got together and caught up a little bit. It was really nice. We were just hanging out a few times a week, seeing movies, and stuff like that. We said our apologies for mistakes in the past, and often discussed where we thought our lives were headed, now that thirty was rapidly approaching, which scared us both.

Taylor had no sort of career, or even one in mind. She would do freelance headshots for people, babysit, and other teenage jobs. She often expressed how great it was that even though I dealt with all this other shit, my career was always an admirable quality.

The movie process was coming along, slowly, but surely. They approved me as a director, which was surprising considering that I dropped out of film school, but I quickly agreed anyway. We were going to start casting soon, and I was using all of my down time reading up on directing. I was thrilled to have the opportunity, but quickly realized that I was in over my head.

I knew some about the directing world, but the more I read, the more I realized that I didn't know the half of it. My only saving grace was that I convinced the investor/producer to hire the same cinematographer that was used on my first film. His name was Malcolm Williams, and I trusted him behind the camera more so than anyone I had ever met. I knew that as long as I could direct the actors, I could trust him to do camera stuff, as unprofessional as that sounds.

My focus was completely dedicated to directing. I spent the nights with Taylor, and the days learning more and more about directing. My agency was able to get me some great opportunities shadowing directors so that I could see the tools I was learning being used first-hand.

The shadowing was great for me. I was able to see how to connect to actors and I received a whole new respect for all the roles on a film set. Everyone's roles were a lot more crucial than I had one time thought they were.

When I wasn't shadowing, I was still working with the producers on the preliminary casting process. We had some ideas for whom we wanted, and now it was time to start putting offers out, something I was not going to really be a part of. These early stages were moving quicker than I had first expected them to, but I knew we were going to be put on hold pretty soon. The way the script was written made it so that it had to be shot in Los Angeles, a decision I made because I didn't want to leave the city in the off chance that Maggie called me.

The issue with filming in Los Angeles was that getting the permits was a nightmare. We finished up the first round of casting, and we had the money in the account, but permitting made it so that we couldn't start production for almost a year and a half. They asked me if I wanted to stick to the script and wait that long, and I told them that I definitely did. I was going to use the time to get my life in order and perfect the shooting script.

Taylor and I really took advantage of my down time. We would go on little trips and adventures all the time. It was nice being able to have Taylor as just a friend finally. There were no weird almost kisses, or who should sleep where's, it was just friendly, and that's exactly what I needed. I always thought I needed more than that from her, but it turns out that's all I ever really wanted. I was never happy with it, because when you are chasing after a goal that doesn't exist, you refuse to let yourself be satisfied. I don't regret any of it, though, because it led me to where I am today.

Dream Taylor would still make appearances occasionally, but it was totally different than it used to be. This new Dream Taylor 2.0, if you will, was the girl I was able to just be friends with, too. The dreams were actually mirroring real life, which was a new thing for me. I know this didn't make me any less crazy, but it seemed like progress.

As time went on, and the dreams still came to me, I knew the next step was to eliminate them. I was shedding the old me to become a man, and this was the last step. I had Taylor in my life in a way that was working for me, and I was starting to feel like I no longer needed that dream world. I was ready to accept the real world, and what it had to offer. I knew the dreams were my own doing, so the only thing that could really put an end to it was me.

We were back at the amusement park, in the food court, having some burgers and beers. We laughed and joked about the last time we were here and how far we had come. I knew this was going to be the last time that I would ever see her, so I wanted to make it a fun day at least. As we sat there, I took her hand, and looked her in the eyes.

— "You know this is it, right? I asked.
— "I know." She told me. She looked sad, but seemed to understand it at least. She clenched my hand back and smiled at me.
— "It's been a hell of a ride." I told her. She looked at the rollercoasters surrounding us and chuckled.
— "It sure has." She responds. I raise my glass and cheers her. We finished our beers and threw our trash out. We got back in line for another ride and continued on with our last day together.

The only real work I had to do in the next year or so were rewrites, and I had already started on them a little. I kept the same idea throughout the script, but I expanded a little. I really made it a flashback of my own life, but I went beyond what I knew. I had always said that you aren't a man until thirty, and your real growth period is between fifteen and thirty, so that's what I expanded it to. I could accurately use my own experiences up until twenty-seven, but I had three years to forecast my own life, and that is what I started doing.

The only work I was getting done was still just rewrites as the production was at a standstill, but that was fine with me. I usually hated the rewriting process, but this time I was really appreciating it. I was more proud of the work I was doing on these rewrites than I had ever been of my writing. I was thinking to myself everyday that this was the project that, no matter where my career went, I wanted to be remembered by.

Things were about to really get started on the film, so I was cherishing the time off as much as possible. We had a meeting coming up that was really going to kick-start everything, so I just waited patiently, polishing my dialogue, etc. I knew this was going to come together in a beautiful way, so rushing it was the last thing that I wanted to do.

The meeting was with almost all of the production team, lead actors, and, via a webcam, the money guys from another country. They wanted to speak with everyone one last time get a feel of the team before the investors gave us the release of funds. The permits were in check, and production was ready to begin. I was so excited, we were going into pre-production in about a week and then our first scheduled shooting day was in exactly two months.

Taylor and I were still hanging out all the time, but things were starting to get a little weird again. For the first time, it was not on my part, but hers. I could sense a change in her mood recently, and it was all after a conversation we had about a month before. I told her that with everything else in my life lining up, the next step was getting Maggie back, and I asked her to help me formulate a plan. While she did try to help, I could sense her hesitation, and I knew it was not going to be a good thing for either of us.

Taylor asked me to meet her for some coffee, and while I already knew what we were going to be talking about, I agreed. I got to the coffee shop late on purpose, and I guess she had arrived early, because she was already settled in when I got there.

— "Hey you." She said. She motioned for me to sit down in the chair across from her.

— "What's up?" I asked. "Sorry I've been so busy recently. My schedule has just been nuts. Is everything good?"

— "Yeah, everything is great, no worries." She seemed frantic as she rifled words out of her mouth. "I just wanted to talk to you about the Maggie stuff, and your plan."

— "What about it?" I knew Taylor was going to try to tell me Maggie wasn't the one, but I had already made up my mind.

— "Okay, well here goes nothing." She took a deep breath before starting into her impeding speech. "I love you, Thomas. I finally realize that I don't want to lose you. I'm done being childish, and I'm done being petty. I now know that I'm a few weeks too late, but I had to tell you. I don't want to spend the rest of my life without you. You're more than just my best friend, you're my future. Let's just walk away from all of this and start a life together. I just needed to say something before you went to try and get her back."

— "That's not fucking fair, Taylor." I was furious. This was just like her to pull this shit now. "I'm sorry, but while I care about you so much, you aren't my future. Maggie is."

— "Do you not love me anymore?" she asked me, somehow turning herself into the victim.

— "I will love you until the day I die, but that doesn't get in the way of me loving Maggie. I have someone now that loves me, and better yet, lets me love myself. You've done so much for me, not much of it positive by any means, and I thank you for that, but I am never walking out on Maggie again."

— "You wouldn't be walking out on her!" Taylor exclaimed. "It's not too late, until it's too late."

— "It was too late the second I saw Maggie for the first time." I told her. "I love her, and I'm going to do everything in my power to show her that."

— "You've always said that I was your dream girl." Taylor was starting to cry now, mascara beginning to bleed.

— "And I meant it. I meant it to an extent that you will never fully understand, but that doesn't change my answer. In the decade or so that you've dragged me along I have learned to separate my dream girl from my reality. They are two different entities completely for me."

— "So none of it meant anything? I never meant anything to you?" She was full on crying now, the damsel in distress in her natural element.

— "You're ridiculous, you know that? And to answer your question, no. I don't think it ever did mean anything. I cherish the experiences we've had, but they are part of my past now, and I am leaving them behind."

Just then it all clicked for me. I finally understood why I had put myself through everything with Taylor, why I justified all of the ridiculous actions.

— "I often think that when you replay a memory enough times, whether or not it is true, you make it your reality. You weren't wrong all of those times that you told me you just didn't have butterflies. I wanted you to be wrong so badly, that I convinced myself that you were. The truth is you felt that way because that was your truth. I have someone now, someone great, who gets butterflies every time they look at me, or at least used to, and I plan on spending everyday of the rest of my life with her."

— "What happened to the guy who tried to kill himself when I broke up with him?" she asked. I took a breath. I always knew this day would come, but I didn't know it would happen like this.

— "That was a lie." I told her. "I'm so sorry that I've never come clean about that, I just never knew how. I was trying to manipulate you, and I apologize sincerely."

Taylor gulped. She was balling. I had never seen her this defeated. I used to dream of this moment, literally. I used to pray that one day I would be strong enough to walk away from it all, and now that I could, I honestly felt bad.

— "If you really are my best friend like you say, I hope you can eventually learn to remember me in the same light that I hold you in." I told her. "Even after all of this shit."

— "So what? This is it? I'm never going to see you again?" Taylor's tears were beginning to turn into anger

— "Of course you will. Just because I'm not going to end up with you doesn't mean that we can't ever see each other. You've had a monumental impact on my life, and nothing will ever change that." She was shaking her head the whole time I tried to talk.

— "I don't think I can be just friends with you. I don't think I can watch you grow old if I'm not doing it with you." She was barely making her words out through her tears.

— "That's too bad, but I understand. If it ever changes, you know it's not hard to find me." I pushed my chair back and got up from the table. I gave Taylor a kiss on the forehead and walked away.

I felt like such a huge part of my life was finally behind me. Nothing from that point on could really bring me down. I officially felt like an adult, even though I had said that a handful of times before. I left that table on a mission. I was going to get a hold of Maggie, and I was going to spend the rest of my life with her.

I was finally able to say "no" to her. And the truth is it wasn't about Maggie, it was about Taylor. Even if Maggie wasn't in the picture, everything I said stood true. I held on to it for so long, and finally letting it go was the biggest relief of my life.

The rest of the year was spent in pre-production, and then the actual filming of the movie. We only had a week left until we started shooting, when I finally called Maggie again, except this time she answered. I sat impatiently through the rings, until I was pleasantly surprised with a "Hello?"

Maggie sounded hesitant with her greeting, but we ended up talking for a while. I told her I needed to see her, and if after that she never wanted to see or hear from me again, she wouldn't. She said yes to one dinner and we set it up for later in the week. I was nervous but relieved.

Friday was the night Maggie agreed to meet me. I had no clue exactly what I was going to say to her, my plan was to hopefully go with my gut once we started talking. This plan seemed dumber and dumber as eight o'clock approached on the day of. Regardless, I got dressed and met her at her favorite sushi bar.

I was there early, just to be careful. I knew I was on thin ice, and any wrong move would leave me freezing. I ordered her favorite sake and a beer for myself and waited until she got there, nervously power-eating edamame. As I was close to finishing my second bowl I heard the scooting sound of a chair scraping across the floor and I looked up to see Maggie. She looked amazing. She had an energy about her that instantly lifted my mood; it had always been that way.

We started out with just the cliché catching up back and forths, but as we drank a little more, and were finishing up our food, the conversation took the more serious turn that it was inevitably going to.

— "Well I told you to call me when you had figured your shit out. What have you figured out?" She was playful with how she phrased the question, but I knew with one false move, she could walk away from that table in a heartbeat.
— "I figured out what's wrong with me," I told her. She did not look pleased at all with the short-form answer.
— "Thomas, if you're not going to take this seriously, I am going to leave. I've wasted enough of my time with you." She grabbed her purse from the back of the chair as she twirled up from her seat. "Bye, Thomas."

As she began to move from the table, I grabbed her wrist, pulling her back down into her seat just hard enough for everyone in the restaurant to suddenly look at us. She raised her eyebrows as if to say "Okay, here's your chance." I looked around to see if everyone was still looking at us, and they were. I was going to have to do this with an audience. I took a breath and let go of her wrist.

"What's wrong with me? That is a long list, but since you left me, my dad helped me find the core of it. That's right, my dad. I'm a giant man-child, but I hope that you will let me be your giant man-child. The center of all my issues is that I hate myself. I don't really "hate" myself, but I don't think I deserve anybody's love, because one girl, one time, didn't love me. Is that pathetic? It sure is… but it's true. I've let the average teenage experience of your first heartbreak affect every aspect of my life since. I didn't do it knowingly, and I'm not happy about it, but I don't regret any of it. My childish habits and stunted emotional maturity may have led to the mistakes that made you leave me, but they were also behind the journey that led me to that airport. That's where I met you, and I will never regret that."

Maggie was tearing up quickly; I could tell that she was doing everything she could not to break down. I was breaking through; I knew I had to close perfectly.

— "Letting you walk out that night, even though you didn't give me much of a choice, was the worst mistake I ever made. Consequently, it did lead me to here, and it allowed me to have the revelation about loving myself, but regardless, not seeing your face for an extended period of time is bullshit. I want to wake up to that smile, and those clever tattoos every morning for the rest of my life."
— "Was that a proposal?!" She stammered back as she asked me, I could tell she was about to faint.
— "No, that was just an apology. When I finally propose, your name is going to be across the sky."

Maggie lunged forward and kissed me over and over. She was crying hysterically now. Everyone in the restaurant, including the staff let out a roar of applause. Maggie looked around at all the smiling faces, and covered her mouth from screaming. She hated crowds. "You writers always need to turn everything into a scene, don't you?"

After that dinner, we were back to normal again. At first, we set up a bunch of rules and regulations for our relationship, so that we didn't rush into things too fast, but that didn't last long. We weren't technically living together again, but if she wasn't sleeping at my place, I was sleeping at hers.

Even though the film was about to wrap, my real focus was on Maggie. We had a quick three-day break from filming, and Maggie's parents wanted us to come visit. I had not been back to New York since I met Maggie, so I was happy to go with her this time.

On the flight we started to experience some turbulence and the captain announced that it might be a bumpy ride. I began to drink, trying to soothe how scary turbulence is for me, but Maggie declined the drinks I offered her. It was only getting worse, and the whole flight was getting more and more terrified as we continued through the dark, cloudy sky.

After the shaking got more violent, finally we dropped a little through the air and the oxygen masks dropped in front of each seat. While everyone tried to keep calm and put theirs on, Maggie began to hyperventilate. I rubber her shoulder with one hand and put her mask on for her with the other.

— "It's going to be okay, I promise." I told her. I didn't know if this was true, but I needed her to calm down.
— "No, it's not!" She yelled back at me, pulling her mask off. She took another breath. "I'm pregnant."

The turbulence continued to shake the plane and I didn't know what to do. I put her mask back on and kissed the top of her head. We sat there for a few more minutes, clutching each other's hands tightly until a voice finally came over the plane.

"Sorry about that, folks, but we are glad to inform you that it is smooth sailing from here on out. We are out of the choppy weather."

I got up from my seat and headed for the front of the plane, drunk, and still scared.

— "Where the fuck are you going?" Maggie yelled after me, she couldn't believe I was walking away again, even just metaphorically.
— "Bathroom." I responded quickly, and continued down the aisle. I had something else in mind and I was determined.

I walked into the bathroom and splashed my face with water, staring myself into the mirror. "Here goes nothing" I told myself. I walked out of the bathroom and pulled the head stewardess to the side where they keep all the little drinks and shitty food.

— "I need you to do something for me." She did not look pleased with my demanding tone but she continued to listen.
— "I need to use the microphone to talk to the plane." She looked shocked at my ridiculous request.
— "Absolutely not, Sir. That is against regulation. No passengers can use that microphone."

I tried a little more to convince her, but it was to no use. She was not willing to budge. She did, however, have an alternative for me, and I gladly obliged.

We finished talking and I went back to my seat. I strapped into my seatbelt and grabbed Maggie's hand. She was asking me questions frantically, but I didn't respond to anything. I just stared into her eyes until the stewardess' voice came over the speaker again.

— "Maggie Smith, would you take Thomas Doheny's hand in marriage? That is all." The voice cut out and Maggie looked at me with the widest eyes I have ever seen.

— "I told you when I proposed I would have your name across the sky." I smiled at her as she started tearing up.

— "Yes!" She screamed out for the whole plane to hear. Some looked happy for us, some clapped, and others looked angry at us for interrupting their Ipad use. "I love you so much."

I kissed her and took another sip of my drink. This was it, I finally did it, and I wasn't scared, I was so content. Plus, I knew that no matter what, this was definitely going to make a good impression on her parents. And it did.

Our trip was amazing; I was reliving my first few days in New York now as an adult, doing all the touristy stuff, and I loved it. We told Maggie's parents about the proposal, and the pregnancy, and they took us out to what might have been the nicest meal of my life. We were only there for the three-day weekend, so we were making every minute count.

Once we were finally back in LA, I had to put everything I had into wrapping this production, and that was not as easy as I hoped it would be. We were finally closing in on the final day when the lead actor, Mark Samuels, playing me, wanted to talk to me about the final scene. The final scene of the last shooting day was the suicide, and the actor wanted to get it perfect in my eyes since I had rewritten it so many damn times. I agreed to go get drinks with him and talk about it. We met for drinks that night.

We sat at a bar, ordered a few drinks, and he told me about the whole shooting experience so far. He made sure to mention how much he loved the script a couple times. A writer always appreciates a good ego stroke. I told him I was glad he enjoyed it so much, and that I thought he was a perfect fit for the character, an equal ego stroke to a young actor. This was his first major feature film.

We eventually got to talk about love, and life, and our own experiences in the two intertwining fields. I told him all about how happy I was with Maggie, and how special what we have is. He told me about his girlfriend, who surprisingly sounded a lot like Taylor. I told him all about Taylor and I's last blow out, and explained how much of this script was about her.

— "So what is this last scene to you?" He asked me. "You've rewritten it what feels like a hundred times."
— "It's the death of the old me. It's the death of who I felt like I needed to be because of the Taylor girl."
— "Aren't you running away in a way though?" He asked. He was a surprisingly smart kid.
— "It's a movie, Bud." I joked. "It's a metaphor. It's a goodbye in the only way the old me could imagine."
— "So how do I play it?" He asked again. He pulled out a yellow legal pad and a pen to take notes like he was in a class. I took the pen and paper from his hand and tossed them under the table.
— "Imagine you're a caterpillar in hell. You've cocooned, and you're finally ready to spread your wings. This is the goodbye to your old life, the only life you've known. You can fly now. You're still going to be in hell, but you're going to be able to fly now. You're starting over but you could not be more excited to be higher, wiser, and freer."

— "Sort of like getting out of middle school?" he asked me. He thought that was a stupid question but it wasn't.

— "That is exactly what it's like." I told him. He smiled. He grabbed the pen and paper from under the table.

— "I'm going to kill this," he told me with a proud sense of entitlement. I could see the determination in his eyes.

— "I wouldn't have cast you if I didn't already think that." He reached for his wallet, but I shooed him off, paying the bill myself. We both said our goodbyes and went our separate ways.

I was going to drive home, but I was not tired at all. Conversations like that revitalize me, and I knew there was no way I was going to be able to go to sleep yet. I knew where I had to go, so I made a quick u-turn and drove back off into the night.

I drove to the studio where we were filming the movie and I convinced security to let me in the front on work related matters that I had to attend to. I was thinking so much about the scene that I had to go to it, I had to live it.

I got to our sound stage and sat in the living room chair where it was going to happen, but that wasn't enough. I went into the prop room and grabbed the gun. I went back to the chair and sat there for a little, thinking about everything I had said to Mark, and how important this scene really was to me.

Almost instinctively, I slowly raised the gun up and put it barrel first into my mouth. "I can do this," I think to myself, in a dark, dark sense of encouragement. My lips are wrapped around the barrel of a .38 special revolver and my hand is trembling. I keep getting distracted by the cold metal against my lips and the end of the barrel pushing against the roof of my mouth. I try to let my mind go blank and really focus on how I'm going to be able to press down on the trigger, but it's not as simple as I always thought it would be. I'm not sure if I'm ready to die, and the idea that I might want to live is really holding me back from letting myself go. I've always been a worrier, but this time, the time I don't want to have any second thoughts, I do. I guess it makes sense, seeing as death is such a permanent thing, but I really wish my stubborn ass would just get on board with the rest of me that doesn't want to breathe for another second.

"What happens when you die?" I ask myself. I think of all the myths I've heard about the experience and settle on, "you see your whole life flash before your eyes."
The problem is that when I look back at my life, I tend to remember the bad over the good. I'm not an extremely negative person or anything like that, but left to my own devices, I would definitely fall into the category of cynical people. I have always felt that an artist, which I obnoxiously consider myself to be, thrives in a state of misery and heartbreak. This is an extremely unhealthy thought process to grow in, but that never stopped me from doing it. The idea that I work better when I'm miserable or heartbroken has influenced every decision I have ever made. The worst part about it is, it has always proven accurate. If you ask me, I think that every great song, film, and piece of art were created out of someone's heartbreak.

Heartbreak fascinates me. Possibly because it's something I've grown so accustomed to, or it could just be because it's such a powerful emotion. Regardless of the reason why, it intrigues me, it always has. The idea of heartbreak seems so foolish, but go ask anyone who's gone through it, and I promise you, they'll tell you there's nothing worse.

The funny thing about having your heart broken is that the impact it has on you depends solely on your definition of the term itself. Love is love, and what you make love mean will determine who you are in this world.

I desperately wish that the first time I heard about the power of love, I wasn't too young to register it. I wish someone could have told me to watch out, or be careful of those silly four letters that control everything in this world, but, like every other child, a concept so great can't be understood until it is felt. I know children feel love, and from the day you are born, you love your parents, and things like that, but that's not the kind of love I'm talking about. The love I'm referring to is the kind of love that doesn't let you sleep at night. The kind of love that fills empty glasses with whiskey, stuffs ashtrays with cigarette butts until they spill out onto tables, and keeps self-help books in the aisles of stores world wide. The kind of love you wish you had never felt, but wouldn't trade the experience for anything in this world.

When I try to imagine my life flashing before my eyes, all I can see is her, and the old me, and a past that I need to shed. Love has made me who I am today, which is weird because this is the second time I have had a gun in my mouth.

Like most people, I found my first love as a teenager, and that's sort of where my life began to spiral downward. I'm twenty-nine now, and I've only just begun to feel like an adult. Some may say that people mature during puberty, or in college, but I think it takes most people fifteen years to truly mature. The time between the ages of fifteen and thirty really shape who you become in this world. The experiences you have during those years are generally the biggest, most important, and most valuable of a person's life. At least that is the truth for the only person I can really speak for: myself.

So here I am, literally trying to talk myself to death. I feel like such a cliché. It seems like it should be so easy, but now that I'm sitting here, I realize that not one muscle, it doesn't matter how strong it may be, can pull that trigger. The trigger of a gun that you hold to your own head is pulled with your brain.

Maybe this is why people leave suicide notes. Maybe writing it all down just before lets you air out a bit. You leave everything on that piece of paper, and don't have to sift through it all in your head.

The letter itself almost seems like a cop-out to me, though. If you leave a note, you're doing it because you know that whoever finds it is sure as hell going to hold on to it.

Someone's suicide note is not something that gets accidentally recycled with that week's coupons to the local grocery store. A suicide note is the kind of thing that people keep strategically hidden under miscellaneous items in desk drawers for the rest of their lives. When you leave a piece of physical evidence like that, you do not really want to die. You'll be remembered forever, at least by a few, because when they hear what your note said, those words will never be able to escape from their mind. They will haunt people forever, and that's just downright unfair. That is precisely why I refuse to go along with the public's pre-conceived notions of how a suicide is supposed to happen. The people my suicide note would be left to have already heard it. Whether it's "I love you" or "fuck you," I take solace in knowing that my suicide note has been scattered in arguments, speeches, proclamations of love, broken text messages, and vows over the last fifteen years.

"Damn!" I think to myself. "That sounded amazing." I'm the kind of asshole that sometimes gets impressed by the way my thoughts sound in my own head, and that was one of those times.

I finally feel like I've summed up exactly how I feel about the situation, and now I need to make my choice. I can either be a coward and dramatically throw this gun across the room, hoping maybe it will fire and somehow ricochet off something and hit me, or I can just man up and do it.

"Here goes nothing," says the voice in my head. I take one final breath and clench my eyes tight. As I hear the halfway click of the trigger, I brace myself for the explosion that is about to be released from the pistol. When I feel the trigger actually hit the handle of the gun, however fast it may have happened, everything really does flash before my eyes.

That was the monologue for the scene, and oh, how true did it ring, now that I was actually sitting here. I put the gun back in the prop room and closed up the set. I got back into my car and drove home.

I opened the front door cautiously to make sure I didn't wake Maggie up. Henry lay on the living room floor, staring at me, but not moving an inch. I walked into our bedroom and saw Maggie asleep in bed, the light still on. I turned the light off and gave her, and her pregnant belly, a kiss. I got into bed, happier than I had ever been, and dosed off. *"Hey you!" I heard. I whipped around to see Maggie sitting at the table across from me.*

ABOUT THE AUTHOR

MACKENZIE KALISH

Born and raised in Los Angeles, Mackenzie Kalish has grown up around writing his whole life. Both of his grandparents, and his father, are award-winning writer/producers for film and television. A distant relative of poet John Keats, he is currently getting his BFA in screenwriting at Chapman University, where he plans to follow in the family footsteps.

Made in the USA
San Bernardino, CA
13 October 2014